# ANAND V/S ANAND

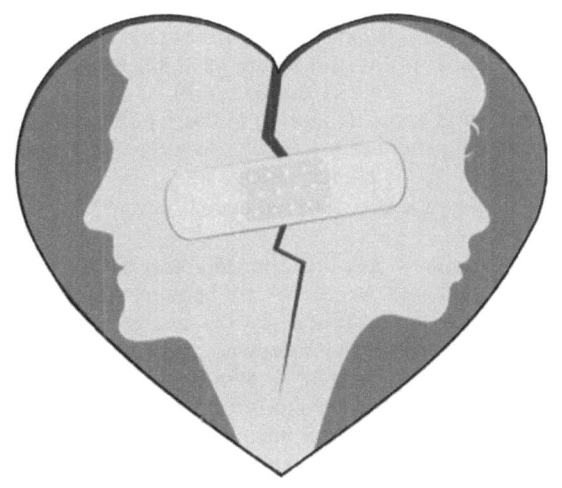

## sukumar mandalika

**First Published in 2018 by**

**Becomeshakespeare.com**

Wordit Content De sign & Editing Services Pvt Ltd
Unit - 26, Building A -1, Nr Wadala RTO,
Wadala (East), Mumbai 400037, India
T: +91 8080226699
Wordit Art Fund helps deserving authors publish their work
by providing monetary support. To apply for funding,
please visit us at
www.BecomeShakespeare.com

©
ISBN - 978-93-87649-12-5

**"LOVE is . . . never having to say you are sorry"**

ERIC SEGAL in his immortal "Love Story"

*"Saanson Se Nahin, Kadamon Se Nahin, Mohabbat Se Chalti Hai Duniya"*

Lyricist INDEEVAR in the Hindi film *"Mohabbat"*

This book is a work of fiction. Its essence - LOVE - is real.

This book is dedicated to TRUE, UNCONDITIONAL LOVE wherever it exists.

author

# 1

"Anand"

"....." here it comes, Anand laughed within himself.

What would it be this time?  A new car?  A holiday in Singapore?

"Anand, are you listening?"

"I'm all ears and yours, Nikita.  Shoot"

"Shoot?  You do all the shooting and..."

"What?  Come again?"

"Anand . . . I'm pregnant!" Nikita said staring at the sea, unable to look Anand straight in the eyes.

"Are you sure, Nikita?" Anand said, only because he had to say something.

"You mean if I'm sure I'm pregnant?  Or if I'm sure it's you, Anand?"

"Don't be silly, dear.  What I meant was..."

"...how did we let this happen? Is that what you meant?" Nikita interrupted "well, darling, this had to happen sometime and it has happened now. What are we going to do about it, Anand?"

*"I'm going to push you into the sea and let you drown"* Anand was tempted to say but ended up saying "I'll take care of it, darling, don't you worry" already beginning to wonder how to end this conversation and this stalemate he found himself in.

"I'm not worrying, Anand. I'm only wondering" Nikita got up and stretched herself before walking back to the car parked far away from the seashore.

"Wondering about what?" Anand asked, as he got up to follow Nikita.

"About whom to go to for the abortion" Nikita said casually, brushing the sand off her dress "I know a doctor who specialises in this, but he charges the sky"

"Are you worrying about money, stupid? Worry about going to the best guy, OK?" Anand chided Nikita, already feeling relieved that there wasn't going to be any stalemate after all, rich as he very much was.

"No more worry now. OK, let's go . . . to the best doctor in town!" Nikita sounded a little too cheerful to Anand.

"Nikita, my dear!" Anand took her hands into his "I'm really sorry to have got you into this, darling. But I'm glad you're taking this so practically!"

"What other option do we have, Anand? Marriage? Both of us know it's no option at all!" Nikita said so casually but correctly "You know I can't leave my father, he's old, he's very sick and has no one else but me!"

Anand got into the car but seeing Nikita go to the ice cream kiosk nearby, got out and joined her. Nikita collected two Cornettos and gave one to Anand.

"What's this, a celebration?" Anand asked.

"No. Just an energy recharge, dear! Celebration will be when I come back from the clinic....free of encumbrance!" Nikita said in a gay mood unusual for a girl in her situation. One hell of a girl, Anand thought, hats off to her!

"Anytime, Nikita. For you, anytime!" Anand said in all earnestness as they finished their ice creams and got into the car.

As they drove back towards the city on the empty highway, Anand noticed that Nikita was suddenly very quiet and brooding. I can't blame her, he said to himself, the kind of ordeals women have to undergo! How lucky to be born a man, Anand thought. How much more lucky that the girl involved is Nikita and not some overly conservative prude "Phew! Closest encounter with trouble" Anand mused as he gave Nikita a bear hug and a parting kiss at their usual meeting point safely away from her apartment.

Anand's phone, kept in silent mode till then, was bursting with missed calls, mostly from his office and from his father. Dad's going to hang me by the neck for sure, Anand cursed himself. He had assured his father that he would meet an important official on business and was actually on his way to meet him when Nikita's call came. What excuse would I come up with this time, Anand wondered and decided that only Mom could come to his rescue as usual. I wonder if even Mom would rescue me if she knew why I missed the appointment, Anand thought as he drove home fast.

# 2

"Asha"

"...." if only I could move faster, Asha thought as she pushed her way through the crowd to reach Sulekha, her friend and colleague in the school, seated at the other end of the bus.

"Asha, come quickly! This seat will get vacant at the next stop" Sulekha shouted over the heads of other passengers lucky enough to be seated, anxious not to have to share the rest of the dreary journey with the foul smelling vegetable vendor woman standing right next to her seat.

"I'm coming, Sulekha" Asha responded "as soon as I can ..." Asha's attention abruptly turned to an invisible hand that was exploring her behind and midriff. The violent jerk that she gave the hand after grabbing it managed to bring into view a young lad too gaudily dressed to be a student. As he nervously tried to free himself from her grip, Asha unleashed a kick that landed accurately on his shin even in the thick of the crowd, as if in poetic justice. The lad rushed out of the bus as it halted at the next stop, wincing in pain with a limp that was as visible as it was amusing to passengers who were privy to this scene.

"Asha, hurry! I'm holding this seat for you" Sulekha shouted, oblivious to the happenings at the rear end of the bus "Where are you?"

"I'm here, Sulekha!" Asha announced, finally managing to dump herself in the coveted seat, exhausted from all the strain and adventure en route.

"What crowds in buses, what population!" Sulekha wallowed "Can you imagine, Asha, how crowded this bus will be five years from now?"

"Right now, all I can think of is how to pay the house rent five days from now! Suresh's college fee is due next month and thanks to mother's lab tests this week, my savings account stands cleaned. It's at times like this I seriously think of lottery tickets and astrologers, then I realise it'll only be more money down the drain!" Asha's mind, already purged of the incident with the lecherous lad, was now agonising over harsher realities of life "But Sulekha, you don't have to go through this hell? Sekhar is ready to buy you a car!"

"And I'm ready to share it with you. It's you who doesn't want to go in a car. Sometimes I wonder if you're really my friend! Don't you ever think of me as your own sister?" Sulekha complained.

"You're much more than a sister to me, Sulekha, you're my only friend! When there is a real emergency, whom else can I go to except to you and Sekhar, dear?"

"Talk of beating you in an argument! Anyway, remember I'm always there for you! By the way, next Thursday is special for me, guess what?" Sulekha was agog with the good news.

"Of course! It's your wedding anniversary!" Asha was quick to answer "It's been seven years now, right?"

"Right, Asha. And to celebrate these seven years of marriage, I'm treating you, mother and Suresh to dinner at your favourite restaurant! Now don't you spoil my mood by lecturing me on economy! What's life without such occasional celebrations?"

"I don't know, Sulekha. I always feel bad when you blow money on us like this. What will Sekhar think of me?"

"He thinks of you as the greatest woman on earth! Sometimes, I even feel jealous of you when Sekhar praises you so much!"

"It is Sekhar who deserves all praise! For being a wonderful husband and for not being a male chauvinist . . you know what . . that most men are!" Asha responded "I would prefer you two to have a quiet evening together. Instead, you're talking of taking a battalion out for dinner!"

"Nonsense! You know both Sekhar & I feel we're part of your family. So, no more arguments on this, OK?" Sulekha ruled firmly.

"OK, Sulekha, you win!" Asha conceded finally "but no going overboard in extravagance. You know all three of us are poor eaters"

"Leave all that to Sekhar. Just don't come up with last minute excuses and spoil the show" Sulekha got up as the bus slowed down at her stop "OK, Asha! See you tomorrow at school"

"See you, Sulekha! My advance congratulations to you and Sekhar! Here's wishing you two will become three for your next anniversary!"

"Keep wishing!" Sulekha blushed as she alighted the bus.

The seat vacated by Sulekha was grabbed by the foul smelling vendor woman. But Asha had bigger problems on her mind to be affected by her new companion. In fact, she even struck a conversation with the vendor woman on the rising prices of fruits and vegetables.

# 3

NORTH STAR CORPORATION with its 9-storey corporate edifice standing tall in a prime business locality was one of the city's most visible landmarks, besides being an immensely successful business organisation. Established in the early 1950's as a trading house exporting condiments and foodstuffs to western markets, North Star today exported commodities as diverse as leather products, garments and now computer software, besides its traditional merchandise. Manned by a staff of more than a thousand direct and indirect recruitments, the corporation's balance sheet would certainly have been a shareholders' delight had it not been a closely held family company.

If it was Anand's grandfather who had assiduously built the company from scratch, it was Anand's father who took the corporation to its present level of eminence with his business acumen and worldly wisdom. Anand himself, after a recent MBA from USA, had only just begun involving himself in this family business, more out of pressure from an ambitious father anxious to pass on the corporate mantle to his only heir than out of genuine interest in this game of power people called commerce.

Anand's mother, like all mothers, doted on her son and just couldn't understand her husband's agony over her son's casual involvement in the family business. She had her own grouse with Anand, though. Much as she tried through techniques ranging from emotional blackmail to plain enticement, she could not get Anand to tie the marital knot to any of the brides-to-be that she painstakingly selected for him. She often worried whether she would ever become a grandmother in her lifetime and dreaded even the slightest possibility of losing her only son to some obscure social cause if not to one of those innumerable religious congregations that seem to nowadays distract young lads away from a normal career and life.

Anand himself had no intentions at all of enlisting himself in causes religious or social. Nor did he intend getting entangled in wedlock. After fulfilling his academic pursuits with more than due diligence, Anand's interests now lied only in exploring the sensuous pleasures of life, unencumbered by ambition or discipline. While he rambled through the day at office under his father's watchful eyes, he savoured every moment with his friends, especially those of the fairer sex. Weekends and holidays were invariably spent in the company of friends, mostly female, at exotic beaches and hill resorts across the country. If it was not an excursion with his friends, it would be a music concert or a movie that you would find Anand in after office hours. That Anand did not drink or smoke was a tender mercy on his mother. That he condescended to attend office during the week without fail was a favour he did for his father, if only to avoid his sermons. That some of his girl friends were those on his company's payroll was a coincidence that was inevitable. That neither of his parents confronted him on his escapades of pleasure, at least so far, was a pleasant surprise to Anand that only made him more determined to make as much hay as he could while the sun shone on him.

"Anand!" his father's voice sounded more stern than usual on the intercom. "Join me for lunch in my room today at 1 pm. I need to talk to you"

"Dad, why can't we talk at home? I always have lunch with my staff at the canteen, you know that"

"Are you ever at home for me to talk? Don't argue. 1 pm, my room!"

"Yes, boss!"

Obviously, mother knew about this meeting. The lunch she sent from home included some of Anand's favourite dishes. It was indeed a pleasure to have home food for lunch once in a while. Anand's father, though, had more serious things to put on his son's plate.

"Anand, how long have you been attending office now?"

"About a year, Dad. Why?"

"And how long do you intend to just attend office?"

"What do you mean, Dad?"

"I mean, when the hell are you going to stop being an employee and start being boss of the company? Why an MBA from USA if all you're interested in was a 9 to 5 job?" Anand always found his father's admonitions dreadful.

"Dad, we've already been through this at home with Mom! I

need more time to get involved in the company. What's the hurry?"

"If you were pushing sixty like me and had a son who seems to be on a permanent holiday while the rest of the world is at work, then you would understand what's the hurry! Grow up, boy!"

"Dad! We are in different times now"

"Different times, my foot! If your grandfather & I had taken life easy in our times, you'd probably be selling dolls at street corners now like all those necktie salesmen! But that's what your son will end up doing for sure, at this rate!"

"Dad, you know I never miss office. I am totally involved in the Division you put me in. It's just that I need some more time to get into your kind of work, Dad. You'll see!"

"Let me see! By the way, I want you to be present when our American associates are here next week for finalising the software contract that we almost lost. Don't go out of town this weekend, you & I need to meet our auditors to iron out certain points before we meet these Yankees"

There goes my weekend with Shilpa, thought Anand! She'll hang me by the neck for this. If only she had a Dad like mine, she'd probably understand!

# 4

$P$rahlad Kumar Sharma, founder & correspondent of Vikas Vidyalaya, one of the more sought after higher secondary schools in the city, became an academician by accident. After graduation, he pursued his dream of going abroad for an MBA. He even secured admission in a reputed UK college and was about to leave for London when a family crisis forced him to stay back. As the eldest son, he became responsible for his mother and his four younger siblings after the sudden demise of his father on the eve of his departure. While managing his father's textiles business, he acquired his M.A. and M.Ed. degrees through correspondence. He left the family business to his brothers and established a primary school that eventually became a higher secondary school with a steadily growing reputation. Far from being happy about this achievement, Sharma nursed a chronic bitterness about his UK dream being shattered. This bitterness always showed in his attitude towards his school employees. One among them was Asha.

Asha was in a hurry to catch the 5 o'clock bus home to take her mother to the doctor before meeting Sulekha and Sekhar at the restaurant, when she was summoned by the correspondent to his office.

"Sit down, Miss Asha. I have something important to say" the normally grim faced Sharma looked even more sober and unpleasant.

"Sir, I'm late for an appointment with the doctor for my mother and..."

"Sit down, Miss Asha! The doctor can wait, what I have to say cannot!" Asha sat down reluctantly, her mind refusing to let go of the bus that she would now miss.

"You know, I've been planning to shift some of the teaching staff to our new school outside the city. Effective next month, you are transferred to the new school as Head of Computer Education. You will, of course, be given additional allowance to travel this distance. I take it you are happy with this promotion and will do your best there too. You can now go see your doctor, Miss Asha"

"But, Sir! Why me? I mean, travelling 50 kilometres up & down each day with a sick mother at home will be too much for a single girl like me!"

"You know what the alternative is, Miss Asha! This school is already overstaffed. I'm answerable to the board of trustees, you know!"

"But, Sir! My entire household will be thrown out of gear! I'd hardly be able to concentrate on my work if half my time is spent commuting on the bus, can't you see?"

"Miss Asha, you have all of this month to make up your mind. I have made up mine. For you, it's either the new school, or ..."

Asha was too upset to prolong the conversation anymore.

Having missed her bus, she now had to take an auto rickshaw to reach home. The crowd of patients at the doctor's was so big, it was almost 9 pm when she reached the restaurant, alone. Sekhar and Sulekha could not but notice the dullness in Asha's face as she gave them her gift for their anniversary.

"Asha, why aren't mother & Suresh here? And what's the matter with you?" asked Sekhar.

"No, Sekhar. We just got back from the doctor and mother needed rest. Suresh has an exam tomorrow"

"I can understand that, Asha. What I can't is the dullness on your usually bright face! Any trouble with the landlord?" Sekhar, very fond of Asha, was genuinely concerned.

"The school lord Mr. Sharma! He . . . well, I'll tell you in a minute"

"Sure, Asha! First things first. What would you like to have?"

"You decide for me, Sekhar. You know what's best" Looking at Sulekha, Asha asked "How did your day go? If you had attended school today, your day would've been ruined too. How can that devil of a man have a name like Prahlad?"

"No wonder, he's still unmarried. I bet he scares the devil out of whoever he wants to marry" Sulekha joined the tirade "Tell me, Asha, what did he do this time?"

Over a bowl of hot tasty soup, Asha narrated her meeting with the correspondent and the Hobson's choice she now was faced with.

"To be or not to be . . . on that bus! That's your dilemma, isn't it? Now you know what poor Hamlet had to go through,

Asha!" quipped Sekhar, to which Sulekha retorted "Sekhar, how can you be frivolous on an issue like this?"

"Take it easy, ladies! I think I have a way out for Asha, but I will talk about it only over dessert, that is if you two ever get to finish your meal for heaven's sake!"

Dessert finally arrived, but both Asha and Sulekha waited only for what Sekhar had to say.

"Can we now do away with the suspense, Sekhar?" Sulekha asked eagerly.

Just to tease the ladies, Sekhar took his own time enjoying his dessert. "Are you qualified in Java and Oracle, etc?" he finally asked Asha.

"I wouldn't last one day with that demon if I wasn't, Sekhar! Why do you ask?" Asha was getting impatient now.

"Have you heard of North Star Corporation?" Sekhar asked Asha again.

"Who hasn't heard of it, Sekhar?" It was Sulekha's turn to ask impatiently "Would you stop this quiz and come to the point?"

Sekhar had a hearty laugh before coming to the point.

"They have a Software Exports Division which is about to finalise a major contract with a USA company. They'd certainly be needing additional staff to meet the deadlines. That's where you come in, Asha!" Sekhar finally revealed.

"How do you know, Sekhar?" Asha was more curious than excited.

"My company is one of their auditors, remember? We had a

meeting with North Star on this subject last Saturday. I know the Chairman of North Star personally. I also know his son who heads this Division. He's an MBA from USA and a very down-to-earth chap. I'll call him and tell him you'll meet him tomorrow. OK, Asha?"

"Sure, Sekhar! But tell him I'll meet him in the evening after school. The last thing I want now is a lecture from Sharma on discipline!"

"OK, Asha, it's fixed then. You'll meet him tomorrow evening at six. Are you ladies happy at last?" Sulekha just smiled, while Asha was more expressive in her gratitude.

"Thanks a million, Sekhar! What can I ever do without your help?"

"Well, you certainly can board that bus, without my help!" Sekhar quipped, making Asha and Sulekha laugh aloud.

**5**

When the North Star corporate tower was inaugurated ten years ago, a simple kitchen-cum-canteen was provided in the basement for preparation of lunch & snacks for the staff. With the company's diversification into Software Exports, this kitchen-cum-canteen was shifted to the top floor and upgraded into one of the most well equipped food courts in the local corporate world, in keeping with the work culture of software companies worldwide. With an ambience that three star hotels would envy and cuisines that gourmets would rave about, the food court was aptly named "Gourmet". It was the favourite haunt of North Star personnel, especially those from the Software Exports Division, prominent among them being Anand himself. Aware that his having breakfasts and lunches at the office annoyed his mother, Anand made a deal with her that dinners would always be at home with her. Quite often, though, Anand would default on this deal and have dinner too at the office. On such occasions, Anand would carry home a pack of the day's special dessert and present it to his mother. Most of the times this gimmick worked for him.

Anand had just finished dinner at the "Gourmet" and was waiting for the dessert pack for his mother when one of the security guards came to him.

"Sir, there is a young lady waiting for you outside your cabin since evening. She says she must meet you" the guard told Anand.

"Young lady? Is she one of our staff?" Anand asked.

"No sir, she arrived at six today and asked for you. Your secretary sent her to Mr. Ashok Iyer" the guard replied.

"Ashok Iyer, the HRD Head?"

"Yes, sir. After meeting him, she has been sitting outside your cabin since 6.30 pm. She says your auditor sent her to meet you"

"Oh yes, of course! Sekhar's candidate!" Anand recollected "Why did you take so long to tell me this?" he admonished the guard as he began to rush to his cabin. "But sir, you had been with the chairman all evening. Secretary Madam asked me not to disturb you there" Anand didn't wait for the guard's explanation and was already on his way to his cabin.

It was nearing ten in the night and Anand was feeling miserable for havin kept a lady waiting so long. As he approached his cabin in the fifth floor, he found himself at a loss for words of apology.

At this late hour, the entire floor was empty with only a few lights on. Anand could not see the person outside his cabin, seated as she was in a chair with its back to him. It gave him that many moments more for preparing his apology. As he approached the visitor he felt relieved to notice a coffee cup and a plate on the centre table and he mentally thanked the security guard for this elementary courtesy.

Whether it was the noise of his shoes or the fragrance of his perfume Anand could not tell, but the visitor sprang up from her chair when he was a few feet away. What struck Anand at first sight was her arresting beauty enhanced by her simplicity and her disarming smile. Dressed in a simple saree with minimal ornaments, she was attractive in a way so different from all those overdressed and overindulged girls he had had the privilege of courting regularly.

"You must be Mr. Anand, Sir?" Asha said with her smile that made his heart flutter. "Gosh, how can she be so pleasant even after a three hour wait?" Anand thought as he floundered for words.

"My name is Asha, Sir" her voice was as sweet as she was "Mr. Sekhar, your auditor, is a family friend of ours. He suggested. . ."

"Miss Asha!" Anand interrupted "First of all, my apologies for this ghastly situation! I . . . I presumed you would have left after meeting Ashok Iyer. Didn't your meeting with him go well? I'm sorry, Miss Asha, I really am!"

"Apology absolutely unnecessary, Mr. Anand" Asha's grace was overwhelming "My meeting with Mr. Iyer was very pleasant. My appointment seems almost certain. I wanted to personally thank you for everything. I was told you were in a meeting, so I decided to wait for you"

"The pleasure will be all ours to have you on board with us, Miss Asha!" Anand was beginning to find himself on firmer ground with this disarmingly beautiful woman "By the way, Miss Asha, you must be starving. Allow me to take you to our restaurant which serves fine food and..."

"Thank you, Mr. Anand, but I would like to take your leave now. It's quite late already. In any case, the coffee and biscuits which your guard served have been quite filling"

"Are you sure, Miss Asha? I'd feel less guilty if you finished dinner here. The food here is very good, I assure you!"

"I'm sure it is, Mr. Anand. But like I said, it's already late and I have a long way to go"

"Very well then. Let me have the pleasure of dropping you at home. It's the least I can do for you, Miss Asha"

"No, no, Mr. Anand! I'm sure I can get a bus or taxi. Please don't bother. You must be having work to finish" Asha pleaded.

"No bother, Miss Asha. It'll be business cum pleasure! Ashok Iyer would anyway want me to see you before appointing you. I can tell him your interview with me is over . . . . in the car!" Anand said with a laugh. Asha could no longer resist his courtesy and warmth.

It was the first time Asha was riding in a chauffeur driven luxury car and was feeling very awkward sitting next to her boss-to-be whom she had met only a few minutes ago. She was counting the minutes for her to reach home.

"How do you know Sekhar, Miss Asha?" Anand noticed her discomfiture and wanted to put her at ease.

"Sekhar's wife Sulekha and I work at the same school. Our families are very close to each other"

"Speaking of family, who else is there with you at home?" Anand found himself genuinely curious to know.

"I have an aged mother and a younger brother who is doing MBA. My father was a retired civil servant and passed away recently"

"So, your family now depends on you for support! By the way, what are your qualifications, Miss Asha?"

"M.C.A. and GNIIT. I have completed advanced online programs in Oracle. I have been teaching computer application to Plus 2 students for the last four years in Vikas Vidyalaya"

"Then Ashok Iyer will have no problem placing you in my Division! Why the change of job now?" the professional in Anand was now talking

"I've been transferred to the new branch of our school which is too far from the city It would be very inconvenient for me with an ailing mother and a college going brother" Asha explained her situation

"Well, you can forget about the school now. I'll talk to Ashok Iyer tomorrow. You will get your appointment letter in a few days. Did he discuss salary, etc? I hope you find our offer attractive enough!"

"I very much do. This will be my first corporate job. Thank you very much once again, Mr. Anand, I really am grateful to you"

"How grateful?" Anand's naughty mind wondered as he said "Don't mention it, Miss Asha! I'm sure you will enjoy the job and work culture here. You'll have longer working hours here but at least you won't have a sore throat yelling at your students, that's for sure!" Anand laughed aloud and so did Asha.

# 6

The day Asha joined North Star Corporation was also the day the company concluded a huge software contract with an American firm. It was late evening after the Americans left when Anand introduced Asha to his Division and to his personal secretary Mrs Narmada an elderly lady whom the Chairman himself had assigned to Anand, not just to strengthen Anand's hands but also to keep tabs on the Division (and on Anand).

For Asha, the new job was gruelling but challenging and consumed all her energies. The work environment was informal and relations with colleagues cordial. Seldom did Asha reach home before night but her mother, now in better health, managed the household by herself. Their enhanced living standards now included a broadband land phone, Internet connection, mobile phones for all and a motorcycle for her brother. Asha's dinners were often at the Gourmet with colleagues. A car was available all the time to drop Asha and other female employees at their homes after work.

Anand found Asha to be very hard working and to have a natural talent for software programming. The Chairman too got a similar feedback on Asha from Mrs Narmada, along with other reports on the Division. The American contract was completed well ahead of the scheduled period of six months, much to the Americans' delight. More contracts followed and the Division's business grew.

Anand's joy was unfettered. Sessions with his father were free of sermons now. Dinners were invariably at home with his mother. His weekends with friends were now regular and uninterrupted. The only problem for Anand now was the increasing pressure on him from his mother to tie the knot. As much to escape this pressure as to solicit business, Anand made frequent business trips abroad. On such trips, Anand always took a colleague along to handle technical issues. Asha was chosen for one such trip to Singapore.

Asha was anything but excited about her maiden trip abroad. The middle class values ingrained in her made her very nervous of being alone with a male that too in an alien land. Asha's mother was visibly thrilled and regretted not having enough relatives to share this news with. Sulekha could understand Asha's predicament but she saw no problem at all in Asha accompanying Anand whom Sekhar vouched for. With her family's blessings and Sulekha's encouragement, Asha finally took off for Singapore with Anand.

The first three days in Singapore were consumed by gruelling sessions with the client. For all the difference it made to her, Asha could have as well been working in India. By the time the contract was concluded on the fourth day, Asha was too physically drained to think of touring the city. But Anand felt responsible for Asha and insisted on taking her on a tour of Singapore. They returned to the hotel in time for dinner which Anand insisted they have together in the restaurant.

"Asha, I must thank you for all the hard work. I couldn't have concluded the contract without you" Anand said sipping his first hard drink ever, a Bloody Mary recommended by the steward.

"All I did was my job, Sir" Asha replied over fresh fruit juice

"Asha, stop calling me Sir. You make me feel like a . . . a boss!"

"Well, you are my boss Sir, aren't you?" Asha quipped

"Well, not now, not in this restaurant. Please call me by my name"

"OK, if you insist, Anand! But only in this restaurant"

"By the way, did you call your mother and talk to her?"

"I did, Sir. I mean, Anand! She's fine. She is eagerly awaiting my return. So am I, I'm missing home very much" Asha confessed and enquired "Aren't you missing home, Anand?"

"Frankly, no! I wish we had a few more days here"

"You like Singapore so much?" Asha was surprised

"No, not Singapore. What I like is being with you, Asha! Back home, I can hardly get to talk to you personally!" Anand, almost done with his Bloody Mary, was becoming less inhibited in his conversation

Asha, embarrassed and not knowing what to say, remained silent.

"Asha, why don't you say something?"

"Mr. Anand, I think we should finish dinner and return to our rooms"

"What's the matter, Asha? Don't you like being with me?"

"Anand, please! Let us stop this conversation. I think I'll have my dinner in my room" As Asha got up to leave, Anand grabbed her hand and pulled her back. Asha was furious at this physical contact, but restrained herself from making a scene

"Asha, I'm sorry! I didn't mean to hurt you. The food is on its way, so please don't leave!" Anand was stunned by Asha's reaction and for the first time was on the defensive with a female. Both of them had their dinner silently. Dessert was being served and Anand, after his second Bloody Mary, could not suppress his feelings anymore.

"Asha, I must tell you something! Ever since I first saw you, I was attracted to you very much! I felt you were the girl for me! I . . ."

"Anand, please stop! This is very embarrassing!" Asha was angry

"It's true, Asha! I always felt thrilled whenever I was close to you at the office. I've never felt like this before with any other girl, and I know a lot of girls. I think . . . I think I am in love with you, Asha!"

"Stop it, Mr. Anand! You're drunk and don't know what you're saying!"

"I know what I'm saying! Right now and here, I've just decided to marry you, Asha! Did you hear? I have decided to marry you!" Anand felt he finally got the better of her. It never occurred to him that he was now volunteering to give up the one thing he had been coveting all his life . . . his bachelorhood, his very freedom.

"Stop it! How dare you?" Asha found it impossible to remain there and abruptly left for her room, leaving Anand gaping at her in disbelief.

From the time she left the dinner table till the next evening when their flight to India was due, Asha steadfastly ignored Anand's persistent phone calls. As she was getting ready to leave the room a waiter delivered a packet and a note. The packet contained Swiss chocolates and the note said "I am very sorry, I really am. What happened yesterday will never happen again, I promise. Anand" Asha threw the note and the chocolates into the dust bin.

Asha remained silent and aloof throughout the drive to the airport. On the flight, she chose a seat far away from Anand's. Anand's chauffer was ready with his car at the airport back home, but Asha hailed a taxi instead.

"It's Friday today. You can take the weekend off, Asha. I'll see you at office on Monday, OK?" Anand tried to make their parting as pleasant as possible.

". . . ." Asha's grim silence told Anand he had failed to repair the damage done at Singapore. As Asha's taxi sped away, Anand's excitement of securing a lucrative contract was competely doused by Asha's rude rebuff. For the first time in his life, he dreaded the prospect of going home to his mother who would right away sense that something was wrong with Anand. After dumping his luggage and the chauffer at the portico, he drove off to a movie multiplex to spend the rest of the day there all alone. Leaving his mobile phone in the car, Anand made sure he was not reachable.

# 7

Before leaving for Singapore, Anand had arranged with Sapna to spend the weekend at a beach resort when he returned. First thing he did after landing was to call off the outing, something he never thought he would ever do. The weekend had already become a nightmare for him.

Anand was seething with indignation of being rejected by a girl. So what if she was a beauty? She worked for him after all! But what infuriated him most was that he still craved for Asha. He wanted to strangle her as much as he wanted to embrace her. Anand was desperate for someone to bail him out of this embarrasing predicament. He first thought of talking to his mother, then remembered and called the one person who he believed could set right things.

"Sekhar!" Anand almost shouted "Anand here. I need to see you right away. It's personal. And urgent. Meet me in ten minutes at the Country Club. Please!" Without waiting for Sekhar's response, Anand rushed to the Club ignoring his mother's appeal for lunching with her.

Sekhar and Anand were close friends from school days. Careers had separated them after college. Business united them recently. Sekhar listened patiently to Anand and began thinking of the remedy even before Anand had finished. First, he had to make sure Anand's was love and not infatuation before trying to convince Asha, something Sekhar knew would be anything but easy.

"Anand, I'm so glad you confided in me. But you must remember Asha is a middle class girl. She just isn't exposed to your kind of society. You must be patient. And, for heaven's sake, Anand, when did you of all people start drinking? Which girl would like it when a guy says I Love You over a drink, even if he's her boss?"

"I made an ass of myself, I know. Want to know why? I was scared, can you believe it? For the first time in my life I was scared talking to a girl! I was always told booze gives you the strength to talk anything to anyone, so I drank for the first time! But I'll never touch the stuff again, that's for sure! I need you to get me out of this mess, Sekhar! I have to talk to Asha . . . very badly, Sekhar!"

"Of course, Anand! Leave it to me, but give me time. Keep your Dad & Mom out of this for now. Attend office and be normal, OK?"

"Sure, I'll try being as normal as I can. Thanks, Sekhar!" Anand gave Sekhar a bear hug out of sheer relief.

Around the same time Sekhar was counseling Anand, Sulekha was with Asha at a nearby restaurant on the same errand.

"For heaven's sake, stop overreacting, Asha! How can you quit your job over such a silly issue? Think of your mother and brother and ignore what your boss did in Singapore!"

"Ignore? You should have been there, Sulekha! He was drunk

and had the cheek to declare marriage! Did he expect me to kneel down and say yes? He hardly knows me, Sulekha! Just because I work for him. . ." Asha was furious

"Calm down, Asha! For all you know, Anand must be eager to say sorry! I'll ask Sekhar to talk to him. They're both friends, remember?"

"I just can't face him on Monday, even if he says sorry! I'll go on leave for a week, then we can decide. OK?"

"OK, but don't act in haste. Wait for Sekhar to talk to him, OK?"

"OK, grandmother! Can we leave now?"

"No! Not until you buy me a Double Sundae!" Sulekha could cheer up Asha even in her worst mood.

The first thing Anand wanted to see at office on Monday was Asha at her desk. Instead, he saw Asha's leave letter placed on his. The next three days were most agonising for Anand. While the rest of his Division was agog with the Singapore contract, Anand was lost in his own private hell. At home, his attempts to be extra jovial with his mother only made his moroseness more obvious to her.

On the fourth day, when the agony became unbearable and Anand was about to abscond from office, he got the call from Sekhar he was waiting for. The cheer in his face as he spoke to Sekhar was visible to every one. It diminished a bit when he learnt Sekhar and Sulekha would be present for his meeting with Asha that evening. Anand spent the rest of the day at home planning what to wear and what to say to Asha.

Sekhar chose a newly opened mall on the city's outskirts for the meeting, mainly for its discreet location. Anand reached the place an hour ahead of the others and utilised this time to buy a gift for Asha. He chose Eric Segal's "Love Story" but not knowing Asha's preference bought the paperback as well as the DVD, got them gift wrapped and complemented them with two roses, one red and one yellow. Thirty minutes and three *cappuccinos* later, as Anand began to wonder if Asha had changed her mind, Sekhar called him to join them in the roof top restaurant.

In spite of having enjoyed the company of girls of all hues, Anand found he was a bundle of nerves. All he could do about it was pray for a happy ending with Asha.

After formal introductions and general chit chat, Sekhar unobtrusively left the table. Sulekha followed him shortly and equally subtly, leaving Anand and Asha all by themselves. But for Sulekha's stern tutoring the whole day, Asha would have left the table too.

Anand found himself fumbling for words again, while Asha sat staring at the empty glass of juice she was holding. Still groping for the right words, Anand called the waiter and ordered a refill for Asha which she did not object to. Taking the cue, Anand launched into his well rehearsed self defence.

"Asha . . . I mean Miss Asha! Thank you for agreeing to meet me" Asha nodded without saying anything

"Please accept this small gift of friendship" Anand said, thrusting the gifts and roses into Asha's hands before she could withdraw them.

"Mr. Anand, why this gift? Sekhar told me you just wanted to talk to me, so I came"

"Asha! First of all, stop calling me Mister Anand. Next, please accept my apologies for what happened at Singapore. I never meant to offend you or take you for granted. I desperately wanted to vent out my feelings for you but ended up doing it crudely, that's all. Let's forget what happened and remain friends, OK?" Anand pleaded with all sincerity

"It's alright, Mr. Anand . . . I mean, Anand!" She could not help being taken in by the genuine feeling of guilt on Anand's face "Let's forget what happened there" Asha said as she put the gifts in her bag

"But Asha, I'd really be happy if you don't forget what I said there!" Seeing Asha silent and pensive, Anand prodded further "Is it wrong for me to have feelings for you? I'm sorry if I shouldn't have expressed them at all, but they were straight from my heart!"

"Anand! Unlike you, I can't afford the luxury of speaking straight from my heart!"

"Meaning, you too have feelings for me, isn't it?" Anand asked excitedly

"Meaning, my heart is elsewhere, that's all!" Asha's reply was sober

"Elsewhere!? You mean . . . you have someone else in your life?" Anand became panicky much to Asha's amusement

"Anand, don't you think of anything else? Yes, I have not one but two people in my life! My sick mother and my younger brother, understand?" Asha was equally amused to see relief return to Anand's face. But all Anand understood was that there was no competition for him and that was all that mattered.

"No, Asha, I don't understand! Everyone has families to look after, but everyone is getting married, aren't they?"

"I don't know about everyone, I just can't get married now!"

"Why not, Asha, why not?" Anand probed aggressively, not willing to let go of the opportunity he sensed

"Anand, we've become friends, but only now. Stop making me uncomfortable, will you?"

"No, Asha, the last thing I'd ever do is to make you uncomfortable. But let's discuss this logically, OK?" Asha didn't respond but that didn't deter Anand "You don't want marriage because you have two dependents. But what makes you think marriage means having to dump them? Even after marriage you can support them, can't you?"

"Anand, don't be naïve! Think with your mind, not your heart! Which husband would accept his wife's family living off her after marriage?"

"This husband would! I'll go one step ahead, I'll support them myself! Believe me, Asha"

"Even if I believe you, Anand, what about your parents? I'm not even sure they'll approve of me, let alone my family! They already have other plans for you, I'm sure. I don't belong to your society, Anand!" Asha tried to put sense into Anand

"They've always had other plans for me, but hey! It's my life, Asha! I decide who'll be my wife and I've already decided" then remembering his faux paus in Singapore, hastily added "of course, only if you are willing, Asha!" Seeing Asha not getting upset, Anand persisted "Please, Asha! Say yes! With you on my side, I can handle my parents and the whole world! Say yes, Asha!"

"Anand, stop getting carried away! I'm not saying Yes . . ." and seeing Anand's crestfallen face, Asha added ". . .but I'm not saying No either! All I'm saying is you should sleep over this. If after a week you still feel the same way, talk to your parents. After all, you belong to them first!"

"Asha, if only you knew who I really belong to! My heart, mind, body and soul belong only to you! But, OK, I'll sleep over this, if I can sleep at all! Say Yes, Asha, say Yes!" If there was any doubt in Asha's mind about his love for her, Anand's appeal removed it permanently

"Anand, I need time too, don't you think? Let's think this over for one week and then decide coolly and calmly, OK?" Asha felt excited too but never let it be seen

"Not OK . . . but OK if you say so, Asha!"

"Now, if you don't mind, Anand, I'll have one more fruit juice!"

"Make that four, Anand!" As if on cue, both Sekhar and Sulekha appeared at the table together, smiling mischievously. Asha was silent but smiling while Anand just couldn't hide his excitement as he animatedly narrated their conversation to Sekhar and Sulekha.

That night Asha who never missed her forty winks even in the worst of times just couldn't sleep. Her heart ached with mixed feelings of excitement and anxiety. As she fell asleep finally, she found herself fervently hoping she would be accepted by Anand's parents.

As for Anand, not even his favourite movies on DVD could take his mind off the debilitating excitement of having won Asha's heart. He wished Dale Carnegie had also written "*How To Win Parents Before Winning Sweethearts*" when sleep finally came to him.

*What transpired that day was that at some point during their conversation, Asha unwittingly surrendered herself to Anand's visibly sincere love for her. It wasn't just Sulekha's and Sekhar's goading prior to the meeting. Neither was it just the passion of Anand's feelings for her. What ultimately played Cupid was the plain truth that a woman's heart beats for a man after all! In this case, Asha's for Anand!*

"Dad!"

"....."

"Dad! Why don't you say something?" Anand persisted.

"What's there to say?  Best of schooling, best of colleges, MBA in USA, future owner of one of the biggest business houses in India and finally? . . . like the rest of the johnnies, my son loves a girl, when he should be loving his business.  I feel terribly let down!"

"I thought mom & you would be thrilled!  After all, weren't you two bulldozing me into marriage ever since I returned?  What's your problem now, Dad?"

"If you knew what my problem was, you wouldn't be asking this stupid question!" Anand's father looked at his wife for a reaction but when he got none he turned his ire on her "How come you don't say anything to your son? Or are you on his side too?"

"I've already told Anand what you've been dreaming for him. And speaking of sides, I think we should at least listen to his side!" Anand's mother responded, with contrasting calm

"And what's his side? OK. He takes one of his employees to Singapore and declares his love for her there. This very ordinary girl rejects him outright! Only after he kneels down before her with a begging bowl does she condescend to consider his love. That's not all! The icing on the cake is that she'll move into our house with her mother and brother whom she will not stop supporting even after marriage! I'm lucky this is just between the three of us, otherwise we would be the laughing stock of our circle! And you want me to give a happy ending to this story?!" Anand was stunned by his dad's offensive

"Dad, I'm the one feeling terribly let down! I never thought you'd be so stuck up on status. Why Dad? Just because Asha works for us? And comes from a different background?"

"Yes! Now don't you start believing all those movies you watch, where anyone can marry anyone and live happily ever after! Such things just don't happen in real life! Can you imagine that girl in our society? What would all our people think of her? And us?"

"Why should I care what they think of her, Dad? Is she marrying me or them?" Anand was furious

"Listen, boy! Like it or not, you have a responsibility to your business, to your parents . . . to us!"

"And you have a responsibility to me, Dad! Please let my marriage be my personal affair, don't make it your business! Meet Asha just once, then you'll see she's as good as anyone in our circle!" Anand blurted and then realised the enormity of his challenge. The silence in the room was deafening to Anand.

"Very well, Anand!" Anand's father announced finally "I will meet this girl, only because your mother wants to meet her too. Call her for lunch this Sunday with her mother and brother. I'd like to see this episode through as quickly as I can!"

"This isn't some TV episode for you to see through, Dad! This is my life. I hope you'll give it the respect it deserves. Anyway, thank you, Dad . . . and Mom!" Anand said hugging his mother in relief

Sunday noon came and Anand realised he had thanked his Dad in haste. Unlike his Mom who was her usual calm and pleasant self, his Dad was moody and irritable all through the day. He was now fervently hoping Asha did not turn up at all. But at the stroke of noon, the chimes of the front door bell ominously announced Asha's arrival.

If Anand was hoping that Asha did not turn up, Asha woke up praying that this day did not dawn at all. All of Sulekha's coaching and Sekhar's counseling failed to exorcise Asha's fears. Until she arrived at Anand's home, Asha barely managed to resist the urge to rush back home. Only after pressing the door bell did she finally decide to go through the ordeal come what may.

Expecting a stiff lipped servant, Asha was relieved to see Anand himself open the door. As Anand dragged her to a corner for last minute advice, she realised Anand was more nervous than her. This amused Asha and made her feel stronger now.

After the formal introductions, Asha presented a small sandalwood idol of Lord *Ganesha* to Anand's mother, an idea of Sulekha's which seemed to have had the desired effect going by the smile it evoked from the recipient. But as Anand reminded her at the front door, it was his father who was the real hurdle and litmus test. As Anand's father walked into the opulently furnished drawing room, Anand noticed Asha's dress for the first time and felt relieved. An expensive but sober silk saree, a thin gold chain, ear rings and long, well groomed hair made Asha a picture of beauty and grace. Even Dad should be impressed, Anand assured himself.

"So, you're Miss Asha!" Anand's father began with an unwarranted air of authority. Without waiting for an answer, he asked "I hear you are working in our Software Exports Division, Miss Asha?" "As if you didn't know!" Anand wanted to cry out aloud.

"Yes, sir! For the last six months" Asha replied politely

"And what does your father do, Asha?"

"My father was a retired government employee. He died two years back. My mother and younger brother are with me" Asha replied

"I see. Your brother, is he employed?"

"He is in his final year MBA, Sir. He should be employed next year, hopefully"

"So, the burden of your family is on your shoulders now?"

"I wouldn't call it a burden, Sir, but yes, they are dependent on me right now" Asha was quick to respond

"What if you were to suddenly lose this job?" Anand's father sprang a surprise

"Well, I would look for another job, Sir. It wouldn't be too difficult, I'm sure" Asha replied after hesitating initially

"How's your mother's health now, Asha?" Anand's mother butted in as she began feeling the heat of her husband's intimidation

"She' quite OK madam, thank you!" Asha welcomed this diversion

There was no further talk until they adjourned to the dining hall. The grandeur of the furniture was matched by the opulence of the cutlery on the large dining table. The food too was rich in variety and taste, but Asha just nibbled at her food, intimidated as she was by the surroundings and atmosphere.

"Asha, Anand tells me he wants to marry you. Do you feel the same way about him too?" Anand's father asked abruptly

Dragged into conversation suddenly, Asha took her time to respond "well, Sir, it was Anand's idea which I did not react to at first. But now, I feel the same way too, Sir"

"Do you think you know Anand well enough to marry him, Asha?" Anand's father continued probing

"Frankly, no, Sir. But I believe his feelings for me are genuine, so I see no problem there. In any case, most marriages are between strangers who spend their lifetime getting to know each other!" Asha was defending herself very well, Anand thought excitedly

"In your case, Asha, not only Anand but his society too is a stranger. Don't you think you have a problem there?" Anand's father fired another salvo

"A challenge, yes, but certainly not a problem, Sir! I presume that behind all the opulence and aristocracy, people of your society too have the same feelings and emotions as mine, don't they, Sir?" How does Asha manage it, Anand wondered as he fought an urge to get up and embrace her.

"You may be able to face this challenge, but do you think your mother would? I mean would she be comfortable in this household and in our society, Asha?" Anand's father remained in war mode

"I don't understand, Sir! Where does my mother figure in all this?" Asha was genuinely surprised

"Wouldn't your mother move in with you after marriage?" Anand's father too seemed surprised

"I wonder how you got that idea, Sir! I'll continue supporting my family, but I certainly won't be bringing them into your house, if that's what you mean, Sir!" Asha was beginning to get weary of the conversation now

"That brings us to the main problem . . . your continuing to support your family! I take it you mean you'll continue working at the office along with Anand even after the marriage?"

"Of course, Sir. I will have to work until my brother is ready to take up the responsibility himself" She looked inquiringly at Anand who just nodded

"Asha! Have you ever thought of my family's image? My daughter-in-law going to work for a salary, that too in my own company? Thankfully, I'm in a position to maintain not only your family but dozens of other families too!" Anand's father could no longer conceal his vanity

"Thankfully, Sir, my father taught me to stand on my own feet and not be a burden on anyone else!" Asha was now visibly indignant

"How can Anand and I be anyone else to you? Can't you see your family will not be a burden at all on me?"

"It certainly will be a burden on me, Sir, if my family begins to depend on you!" Asha's anger now reflected in her face and tone

"Asha, now you're being impertinent! Here I am talking practically about the marriage and you're taking this emotionally! What's wrong with your family moving into our house after marriage, unless of course they will find this house too small for them?" the sarcasm in his words were not lost on Asha

"I'm not being impertinent, Sir! It is you, who's being impractical by suggesting that my family depend on your benefaction instead of my salary" Anand shuddered to look at his father's face at that moment, knowing his ego well

The conversation came to an abrupt halt. Anand's father realised he had to digest not just the food on the table but also the belligerence of the visitor sitting across it. Anand's mother indulged in small talk to ease the tension. Anand just focussed on his food praying for a truce, while Asha exchanged pleasantries with his mother for the rest of the time. When Asha decided to leave, Anand and his mother walked her to the front door. Seeing Anand's father seated in the living room, Asha walked back to him to take his leave.

"Sir, I apologise if I have hurt you, but it was necessary for me to be completely frank. I know a middle class girl like me would not be the natural choice for Anand. This marriage will not take place unless you and mother accept it wholeheartedly. It's been an honour to have met you and mother. I will take your leave now, Sir!" Asha bent down and touched his feet before leaving

This time, to Anand's and his mother's amazement, Anand's father not only walked Asha to the door but personally instructed his driver to drop Asha at her home.

It was late evening when Anand's father completed the work he brought home from office. Over a leisurely cup of tea, he conferred with his wife for a long time before summoning Anand. Anand's anxiety vanished the moment he read his mother's eyes that revealed her joy. Anand hugged her, then hugged his father. Then, for no apparent reason, he cried like a baby for a minute before blurting "Thanks Dad! Thanks Mom! I love you both very much!"

"Anand, listen carefully. Your mother & I are convinced Asha is the right girl for you. Perhaps too right for you! I'm sure she'll do everything to make your life happy. But today, I want your word that you will do nothing wild or stupid to wreck your marriage!"

"Dad, what do you mean?" Anand was taken aback

"Oh, come on, Anand, you know what I mean! Your weekends and outings with all those girls were your private affairs till now. But after marriage, these will have to stop!" Aghast, Anand blurted "Dad, I . . ." but his father continued "Don't worry, Anand, we won't go into all that. But today I must have your word you will behave yourself! I'm sure Asha believes she's the only girl in your life. From now on, I

47

want it to be strictly that way!" Seeing Anand dumbfounded his father persisted "Do I have your word, Anand?" with his mother watching Anand's face closely.

"Dad, Mom. You have my word! I love Asha and Asha alone!" Anand declared with a flourish.

Anand's message to Asha's mobile phone later that night said it all: "Why isn't your name Jhansi Lakshmibai? Or Joan of Arc? Or Margaret Thatcher? Mom & Dad are your fans now! I've always been one! Congrats, my dearest!"

# 10

It took all of Sulekha's and Sekhar's cajoling, Anand's appeals and finally her mother's admonishing to make Asha concede to a pompous wedding planned by her father-in-law. "It's their money, Asha, why should it bother you how they spend it on their only son?" Asha relented to her mother's simple logic, though she could not condone the vulgar display of wealth that marriages had now come down to. "What real purpose can this meaningless extravagance serve? Can you imagine how many hungry mouths can be fed with this money, and for how many days?" Asha lamented apparently to no avail.

In a befitting response to Asha's rationale, Anand very discreetly organised free meals for the inmates of all orphanages and old age homes in the city, more than fifty of them, for all the three days that their wedding rituals had lasted. When Asha learnt this from Anand himself on the post wedding reception dais just before the guests began to arrive, she rushed to her room. Puzzled, Anand waited outside her room for ten full minutes before Asha emerged. With a freshly made up face that still betrayed signs of tears shed copiously, she pulled Anand into her room and gave him a bear hug that puzzled him even more "Anand, you couldn't have given me a better gift than this for our wedding. I love you!" Asha cried again.

The wedding ended in great pomp and pageantry that left Anand's parents thoroughly gratified, Asha's family thoroughly amazed and the newly-weds thoroughly exhausted.

When time came for the couple to leave on their honeymoon, Anand managed to keep Asha guessing about the destination till it was their turn at the check-in counter in the airport. Asha's joy knew no end when she discovered that she would be spending the next ten days in Singapore, in the same hotel she was with Anand the first time. Only this time, the two would be together in the penthouse suite reserved for couples on honeymoon.

Both Anand and Asha had lost track of time. For Anand, not even his wildest escapades in the past compared remotely to the happiness he derived with Asha. He realised only then that there were pleasures more ecstatic and fulfilling than mere carnal experiences "Now I know why they say marriages are made in heaven!" Anand mused aloud on the second night as he lay satiated in Asha's embrace and drifted into deep sleep.

For Asha, it was literally being reborn into the world, this time as a complete woman. Every morning she would wake up to the fact that she had been an incomplete person till then. "Where were you all these days, Anand?" she would ask his tranquil sleeping face before falling asleep herself.

When the time came, it was difficult to judge who between the two was more reluctant to return home. It was equally difficult for the two to retrieve themselves from the dreamy world of ecstasy they had discovered and return to the dreary world of reality.

# 11

"Anand!"

"Yes, darling!" nothing sounded sweeter to Anand's ears than Asha's voice, especially on phone. But not at that moment, engrossed as he was with an important client "Can't this wait till lunch?"

"I'm at home now, Anand, not in the office"

"What? Why?" Anand was surprised because they had come to office together like they always did.

"That's what I want to talk to you about! How soon can you come home?"

"Asha! For God's sake, are you alright? Put mom on the phone!" then as an afterthought "Or is it mom who's sick?"

"Anand, there's nothing wrong with mother or me!" Asha managed not to betray her amusement at Anand's panic "Get home as soon as you can!" she said trying to sound serious.

Anand was a bundle of nerves when he reached home earlier than usual. He was praying nothing was wrong with anyone. He did not know what to make of Asha's smile as she opened the door for him. Nor did his mother give any inkling of what the matter was as they assembled for tea. Only when he was alone with Asha could Anand give vent to his anxiety.

"Asha, stop playing games. What is it?" Asha was teasing him with her smile "Can you imagine what I've been going through since you called?" Anand was visibly angry

"Anand! Would you stop loving me if I became fat and ugly?"

"What? Is this some kind of a joke? For heaven's sake, can't you tell me . . ."

"No joke, Anand! I am going to become fat and ugly like all other girls do! It's happened to your mother too once!"

"Why, what happened to my mother? And what . . ." suddenly the answer came to him like a flash "Hey! Don't tell me . . . you're going to be a mother?"

"You're going to be a father, Mr. Anand!" Asha finally broke the news "My giddiness and nausea increased at office today so I went straight to Dr. Sheela. She confirmed the good news!"

Anand grabbed Asha and filled her face with kisses "Did you tell mom about this?" he asked Asha as she struggled to get out of his embrace

"No, we'll tell mother & father together!"

"Right away, darling! But first, get dressed. You & I are going out to dinner after breaking the news to them!"

"No, Anand! I just don't feel like eating any food right now!"

"Nonsense! You can eat ice cream, can't you? The baby will

love it! From now on, don't you dare starve my baby, is that clear?" Asha enjoyed Anand's admonition as much as his excitement.

After a mini celebration at home with his parents, Anand drove straight to Asha's favourite restaurant, stopping en route at a supermarket to buy some flowers and chocolates for the mother-to-be. Asha was pleasantly surprised to find a large cake with a candle already placed on their table. Even more surprising was the sudden entry of Sulekha and Sekhar along with Asha's mother and brother who were discreetly tipped off by Anand from the supermarket. The loud and warm celebration that followed was something Asha would cherish forever.

"Anand, if this is the way you're going to feed me everyday, I'm sure to become fat and ugly! Then, you'll surely leave me for someone else!" Asha kept complaining from the time they left the restaurant till after they slipped into bed.

"No problem, dear! After the baby is born, remind me to cancel all your meals for the rest of your life!" Anand quipped in happiness.

"I don't know about tomorrow, but today is the most beautiful day in my whole life! Thank you, God!" Asha kept telling herself for the rest of the night.

# 12

"Asha!"

"Yes, Anand?"

"How did the check up go? Did Dr.Sheela say the baby is OK? What about your bulging feet? Has she . . ."

"Anand, stop worrying about me, for heaven's sake! Of course I'm OK! Don't you have any work to do at the office?" Anand's indulgence always made Asha blush

"Thank God, Asha. Now I can get back to work. Talking of work, I have good news. Guess where I'm off to the day after tomorrow? Singapore! For one full week! One more contract!"

"You'll be away for seven days and you call it good news? You know what, Anand? I think you already find me fat and ugly, that's why it is good news to you, isn't it?" Like most pregnant girls, Asha found herself becoming petulant and insecure as the months progressed.

"Don't be silly, Asha. You know I like nothing more than being with you. But this is important business. I even asked Dad to send someone else, but he too felt I should go this time"

"I was just joking! Get back from Singapore as quickly as you can. But first, get back home right now! Your duty's with me, at least until day after tomorrow!"

The last seven months had been unique for Asha. While she was overwhelmed with the pampering by the entire household, she also found it suffocating to remain cut off from the outside world, especially office. Sulekha and Sekhar's visits, though full of fun, always left her feeling lonely afterwards. Anand's company was her only lifeline to sanity, but having to share his time with the office irritated her no end. The growth inside her proved to be a strange medley of physical ordeal and emotional ecstasy. Amid such contrasting moods that all mothers-to-be go through, it took Asha all her resolve and energy to be positive and pleasant. But even in this blurred state of mind, Asha always believed that there could be no better husband than Anand. When not at the office, he would invariably be with Asha, much to his mother's amazement. He would bring home comedy and cartoon movies daily to entertain Asha. He would take her on long drives on the weekends, driving very slowly. He would constantly feed her with exotic ice creams and chocolates on the pretext of feeding the baby. Unless busy, he would himself take Asha to the doctor for monthly checkups. Even his fastidious father could not but appreciate this welcome transformation in Anand, regarding it as a miracle of sorts.

The night before the departure was an emotional ordeal for both Asha and Anand. No amount of Anand's cajoling could take Asha's mind off her premonition about the trip "Singapore is just four hours away Asha, if you & I decide to recall him!" Anand's mother consoled Asha as they left for the airport, noticing neither of them had slept the whole night.

Emotionally drained and physically exhausted after reaching Singapore, Anand took the first day off. After a light lunch, he went to see a Jackie Chan movie playing near his hotel. He enjoyed the movie very much but felt morose once it was over. Remembering the list of things he had prepared on the flight for Asha and the baby, he spent the rest of the evening in a shopping mall. While waiting at the crowded cash counter, he found his purchases too bulky for him to handle and wished there was someone to carry them to the hotel.

"Anand!" A familiar voice from the past made him turn

"Nikita! What a surprise, after all these years! How come?" It was a pleasant shock for Anand to see Nikita

"I never dreamt I'd run into you of all people!" Nikita was equally shocked "On business, Anand?"

"Yes, I'm here for a week. What brings you?"

"I'm based here for the past one year. I'm working for a magazine on IT and computers. I live nearby and buy my provisions and clothes here"

"Great! Is that why you didn't attend my marriage last year?" Anand asked out of curiosity

"How could I? I'd already left India by then. They redirected your card to me here very late. How's married life, Anand?"

"Great, Nikita, great! I can talk for days together on how life with Asha is, but first help me get all this stuff to my hotel, OK?"

"Sure. After that, why don't we have dinner at my place?"

"No, don't bother with cooking today, Asha . . . I mean, Nikita! We'll have dinner at my hotel today"

The chance meeting with Nikita was to Anand a pleasant rendezvous with his carefree past that was only a vague reminiscence now. He was as excited being in Nikita's familiar company as he was while narrating his life with Asha to her. So engrossed was he with Nikita that by the time he saw her off in a taxi he realised it was too late in the night to call Asha. As he fell asleep watching television, he reminded himself to call Asha first thing in the morning.

# 13

$T$he team of doctors operating on Asha looked menacing with their masks and scalpels. Even with all his strength Anand could not overpower the orderly who prevented him from entering the operation theatre where Asha was on the table. As Anand watched helplessly through the glass door, one of the doctors suddenly rushed to a corner and began vigourously ringing a fireman's bell hung there. As the chimes of the bell reached a crescendo, Anand jumped up in his bed only to realise that it was the bedside phone ringing.

"Anand!" Asha's voice was as pleasant as ever though a trifle anxious

"Yes, dear?" Anand was now fully awake from his dream

"You know how worried I was whole of yesterday? Why didn't you call me?"

"Darling, I'm very sorry! It was too late in the night by the time I reached my room. I was to call you in the morning. What time is it?" and noticed that the bedside clock showed eight in the morning.

"It's five thirty in the morning here. I've been so worried! Are you alright?" Asha's anxiety only amused Anand

"Of course I'm alright. I miss you very much, though. Did you miss me?" Anand enquired mischievously

"No I didn't, actually! I was very busy with my boy friend the whole day! Any more dumb questions?" Asha retorted

"Take it easy, Asha! I promise I'll call tonight and every other night I'm here. Now, can I get dressed and go to work, please?"

"Yes, you may. But if you don't call tonight, I'll run away with my boy friend and never come back!" Asha declared in mock seriousness

"Hey, who's this boy friend of yours? Anyone I know?"

"Your son, stupid! It must be a boy, the way he kicks around inside!"

"And you're shameless enough to run off with a fellow who kicks you?" Anand quipped

"At least, he always stays with me, unlike you!"

"Well, he doesn't have anything else to do, while I have a lot of work, especially today! Bye dear, I'll call you tonight to find out how many times you got kicked!"


It was late evening by the time Anand reached his hotel after a really hectic day with his new client. The message at the reception, though unsigned, was obviously from Nikita who insisted that he join her for dinner at her apartment.

Nikita surprised Anand with a simple but delicious meal after which they settled down to watch an old English movie on TV. Nikita had red wine and a cigarette, while Anand ate ice cream. Halfway through the movie, both of them lost interest and preferred to catch up on old times.

"Can you guess why I moved to Singapore, Anand?" Nikita quizzed

"Must have been the money and independence, what else?"

"Living in the same city without seeing you was unbearable, that's why!"

"Are you serious? I never thought you were the sentimental kind!" Anand was genuinely surprised at this facet of Nikita

"I never am. But somehow, in your case I became. I began missing you very much. When our friends told me you were in love with a girl in your office, I felt very jealous and depressed. I got out of the country only to get you out of my mind. But here I am once again, sitting in front of you all alone again!" Nikita poured herself another glass of wine, to avoid gazing at Anand

"Nikita, I don't know what to say . . . it's getting late. I'll see you again" As Anand got up, Nikita jumped up and put her arms around him

"Nikita! I'm married now, for heaven's sake!" Anand protested as he got her hands off him.

"I know that, dammit! Can't you stay tonight? This moment will never come again, you know that!" Nikita's tear filled eyes beckoned Anand, but he thought it best to get out.

"Nikita, it's been great . . . our meeting I mean. Please don't spoil it now like this!" Anand pleaded as he went to the door but seeing Nikita crouched in her chair crying, Anand went back and took her hand in his "Nikita, you've always been a brave girl, what's happened to you now? Cheer up, I'm still your best friend! I'll pick you up by seven tomorrow and then we'll go for a movie and dinner, OK? Good night, Nikita!" Without raising her head she squeezed Anand's hand and mumbled "Good night!"

"Five times!"

"What?" Anand's mind, drifting back to Nikita's apartment where he was until an hour ago, did not register Asha's opening words on the phone

"You wanted to know how many times I got kicked today! Five times!"

Amused and relieved, Anand spoke to Asha for over an hour by which time he got over the incident with Nikita and was ready for a well deserved sleep.

# 14

The slips at the hotel reception every day for Anand for the next four days bore the same message from Nikita. Anand's resolve to avoid her remained the same too. On the evening before his departure, Anand returned to his room earlier than usual to find a gift box instead of a message.

After calling Asha to confirm his return and then room service for food, Anand opened the box. He recognised the articles kept along with a note that said: "May God give you the peace you haven't given me. Goodbye!" The wrist watch and the gold bracelet were the ones he had presented Nikita on her birthdays. On an impulse Anand called room service and cancelled the food. The only way to end this dilemma tormenting him, he decided, was to pay one last visit to Nikita. You don't belittle your past so boorishly after all, he told himself.

With flowers in one hand and the re-wrapped box in the other, Anand reached Nikita's apartment with a strong feeling of guilt. He was debating within himself if it would be wiser to leave when the front door opened.

"So, you finally found time for me? Thanks!" Nikita camouflaged her pleasure of seeing Anand with sarcasm

"Nikita, I'm leaving tomorrow. I came to return this box, it's yours"

"Scared your wife might discover these gifts? You could have told her you bought them for her. Or better still, you could've dumped them in the dust bin like you did my feelings! Why bother coming?" Asha controlled her tears

"Nikita, stop hurting me like this!"

"Oh, so you're the one who's hurt now?"

"Nikita! Let's not spoil our last evening. Take me to the best place in town for dinner!" Anand cut short her whining by leading her to her dressing room

The best place in town happened to be a Japanese restaurant very near Anand's hotel.

"They serve very good Sake here" Nikita said ordering one for herself

"What's Sake?" Anand asked out of ignorance

"It's a Japanese alcoholic drink, made from rice. Want to try one?"

"No thanks, I'll settle for apple juice"

"Boy, you really are married, aren't you, Anand!" Nikita quipped

"I never take alcohol, you now that don't you?" Anand retorted

Discovering that Nikita knew a lot about oriental cuisine too, Anand left the ordering to her. While he hardly finished his glass of juice, Nikita was already on her second Sake.

"Nikita, go slow on your drink, will you?"

"You don't have to carry me home, if that's what you're worried about! I'm used to drinking alone" Nikita became morose, Anand noticed

"But why drink at all, can't you find something better to do?"

"Like you found love and marriage? Everyone isn't as lucky as you, Anand!"

"Now you're being cynical!"

"If the girl you loved had not become your wife, you'd be cynical too!" How true, thought Anand, remembering the trauma he underwent in this very city

"Life doesn't end just because love isn't returned. Be positive, Nikita! You're a great girl. You will surely find someone who'll love you"

"It's easy for men to move on. Women can't do it so easily, but you wouldn't understand!" Anand found Nikita becoming more and more melancholic

"Nikita, if there's anything I can do to make you feel better, I'd. . ."

"If you really mean it, take me to your room right now. Only then can I begin to get you out of my system!"

"Nikita, stop being unreasonable! How can I..."

"You stop being a coward! You . . . goodbye, Anand!" Nikita grabbed her handbag and tried to get up from the table

"Nikita, wait a minute!" Anand caught her hand and pulled her back

"What's the point of being with you and yet not really being with you? I just can't bear this torture any more!" Nikita almost wept

"Nikita, for heaven's sake! Sit down and finish your meal"

While the two finished their meals in silence, Anand brooded on the situation "Nikita!" Anand spoke finally "about getting me out of your system, do you really mean it? I mean, will you stop torturing yourself about me after tonight?" Anand asked, knowing fully how forbidden this question was

"If only you'll give me the chance, Anand, I surely will!"

"Nikita, I'm doing this only because . . . because I can't see you like this! I want you to be happy like everyone else. I feel..."

"Don't feel anything else, Anand! Just feel me!" Nikita whispered as she led both of them to Anand's hotel.

# 15

On the flight Anand tried concentrating on the movie they were showing, but his mind kept darting back to the night before. Though physically satiated, especially after months of abstinence from Asha, his guilty conscience did not let Anand savour the experience. Alone in his row of business class seats, he found himself soliloquising with his own conscience.

"So, you feel macho now like Casanova, eh?" His inner voice seemed so real it was as if his mirror reflection was sitting right next to him "Any idea how Asha would react when she comes to know?"

"Am I an idiot to let Asha know? Don't you know how much I love her?" Anand almost spoke the words aloud

"Oh, so you love Asha, do you?"

"What kind of a dumb question is that? Of course, I do!" Anand retorted

"Yet, you chase another woman at the first opportunity?"

"I didn't chase her, Nikita chased me and you know that!" Anand felt indignant

"What's the difference? You succumbed to her, didn't you?"

"You call it succumbing? I first avoided her then tried talking sense into her, you know that. Dammit, she's my good friend, how can I let her suffer in pain? What I did really was help her get me out of her system and get on with her life!" Anand defended himself

"But you are a married man! How can you keep playing Good Samaritan to every other girl you run into?"

"Nikita is not every other girl, she is special to me. Just because I'm married doesn't mean I have to ignore my old friends. Nikita needed my company badly so I gave it to her! Why can't you leave it at that?"

"Can you leave it at that if Asha were to do the same thing to you?" Anand's alter ego would not let go

"Stop this nonsense, will you?" Anand was furious, but with whom?

"Typical, anything you can't face is nonsense! But honestly, how would you feel if your wife were seeing another man?"

"....." Anand was so irritated he wanted to strangle his inner voice but just didn't know how to go about it

"Well?" his inner voice persisted like a prosecutor does with a law point

"As if you don't know . . . I'd strangle her and the guy!" Anand said hoping this would silence this irritating non-entity

"So? Asha can now strangle you and Nikita, can't she?"

"She can, but she won't! No woman would, that's what makes

women great & beautiful, don't you know?" Anand retorted triumphantly

"No, I didn't know! I thought God created man and woman to be equal!"

"Now, why bring morals into this?" Anand wished his inner voice would leave him alone and find someone else to pester

"Because this is a moral issue! When you married Asha, you got her all for yourself, didn't you? Shouldn't you too give yourself only to Asha?"

"Where's the doubt? Is there anyone else expect Asha in my heart?" Anand found it ridiculous to be proving his love for Asha to his own self

"Asha certainly wasn't in your heart when you were with Nikita!"

"It's easy for you to sit on your non-existent behind and lecture me! Try being a real friend and a true husband at the same time and then you'd know how difficult it is! Anyway, Nikita's is a closed chapter for me now. If anything, this experience has only strengthened my love for Asha all the more! I'd now like to focus only on Asha, if you don't mind!" The moral duel that was puncturing Anand's self esteem came to an abrupt end when the stewardess announced the landing of the flight.

The grim expression on his driver's usually cheerful face told Anand something was wrong. His thoughts immediately went to his parents and hoped they were not in danger.

"No, Sir! Both of them are fine. They wanted me to take you straight to the hospital where madam has been admitted for an emergency delivery" The driver broke the news as calmly as possible but Anand panicked and reached for his cell phone

"Dad! Only yesterday evening, I spoke to Asha and she was fine! What happened now? Tell me Dad, please!"

"Take it easy, boy! Asha's quite OK. She developed sudden pains this morning so we rushed her to the hospital. Dr. Sheela is doing a Caesarean right now. By the time you get here, she'll be back in her room. So, relax, daddy!" In spite of his father's soothing words, Anand was a bundle of nerves as he drove into the hospital with a guilty conscience, praying for Asha and their baby to be safe.

# 16

Anand had only read in books about a father's ecstasy on holding his newborn baby. He now experienced this ecstasy as he held the baby boy in his unsteady hands. Nothing else mattered to him at that truly memorable moment except watching his baby breathing gently with its eyes closed. After a while, a nurse took the baby back to its incubator while his parents ushered him into Asha's room.

Anand brushed Asha's face with his lips and whispered into her ear for more than five minutes before Asha recovered from the anaesthesia and recognised Anand.

"Sorry darling . . . for all the tension I put you through!" Asha said feebly and firmly held Anand's hand.

"Nonsense! I'm the one who should be sorry, for not being with you. Really I am! I..." bursting into tears, Anand hid his face in his hands

"Hey, what's this?" Asha pulled Anand's palms away from his face and kissed his forehead "Stop being a baby, Anand, it's not your fault that I had an emergency"

"You don't know, Asha! I've been very selfish. I should have sent someone else to Singapore. You desperately wanted me to stay with you but I didn't. I'm really sorry dear!" Anand's apologies only amused Asha

"Don't be stupid, Anand. You're running a business and you had to go. Father too felt so, didn't he? So stop worrying ... and start enjoying being a father! Or, are you already sorry you're one now?" Ever when semiconscious, Asha enjoyed teasing him

"Now you're being stupid! When I held him in my hands, I felt as if I owned the whole world! Thank you so much for giving me the best gift on earth!" Anand tried kissing Asha passionately, but she pushed him away firmly "Stop it Anand, I haven't brushed my teeth! And behave yourself, you're in a hospital! Now, go home and get some rest. Come back in the evening! Or, why don't you go to the office?" Asha suggested

"Office? This room is my only office till you get discharged, is that clear?" Anand admonished her

"In that case, Anand, I'll ask father to sack you!" Asha quipped "There are nurses & doctors here, in case you haven't noticed! Both our mothers are with our baby, so we don't need you here!"

"Hey, how come we haven't yet decided on a name?" Anand wondered suddenly "Start thinking of one, now that you've nothing else to do!"

"I will, if you promise to go home and then to office. You've been away for more than a week! See you in the evening, darling!" Asha felt drowsy so Anand left her and went home along with his father.

Anand reached home but rest was the last thing on his mind. He called up office and asked for their interior designer to come home right away and then began freshening himself up. By the time the designer reached home, Anand was brimming with ideas on how to decorate the baby's room. After lunching at The Gourmet first, Anand spent the afternoon in office. He rushed through his briefing to his colleagues on the contract before returning to the hospital.

"Darling, don't you know I can't eat such things right now?" Asha laughed at Anand seeing him walk into the room with a bag full of cakes, cookies and chocolates

"Who says so?" Anand asked defiantly

"I say so" Anand's mother entered with the baby "and so do doctors everywhere! Don't you know puss forms around the sutures if she eats such stuff?"

"How can I know, mom? You eat them, then!" Anand stuffed a cake into his mother's mouth "Congrats, mom! For becoming a grand mom when you still are beautiful enough to be Miss World!" Asha always enjoyed Anand's camaraderie with his mother

"Save your compliments for Asha and the baby! But remember you have only five minutes with your son before he goes back to the incubator" Anand's mother cautioned him as she went out of the room

"Incubator, why?"

"Because your son is two weeks premature, that's why! Wait till he gets home and then he's all yours!" Asha clarified

It was only on the fourteenth day that Asha got discharged along with the baby. Anand was in a real hurry to get home, but Asha's mother insisted they first visit a temple. Asha wondered why Anand was so anxious to get home. She got her answer when she reached there.

"My God! Whose room is this, Anand?" Asha exclaimed after seeing the baby's room with its breathtaking colours and beautiful toys spread around the cradle

"Your son's, stupid!" Anand declared proudly "By the way, did you decide on the name for him? All I've done in the last ten days was eat and . . ."

". . . and sleep?" Asha quipped "I have chosen a name, but I'll reveal it only during the naming ceremony. You come up with yours and we'll let father and mother choose one of them!"

"As you like it, my lady Macbeth!" Anand went Shakespearian in joy

# 17

Neither Anand nor Asha noticed the next two years fly, so engrossed and enchanted were they with their son, who was named Arjun after the grandparents backed Asha's choice which was among the names Anand had short listed too.

Anand wanted Asha to work as much as he wanted her to raise their baby, convinced that Asha's skills in software were too good to be wasted. Thus it was that one of the many vacant rooms in their home was converted into a full fledged office for Asha complete with Internet and all the allied gizmos. Anand's father was amazed at Asha's astute handling of both her roles, while his mother came to her rescue whenever the need arose. Asha's brother was now employed in a multinational company in the same city and was doing well enough to buy a flat for himself and look after his mother. Sulekha and Sekhar often visited the Anands but spent most of their time with the baby. Barring the occasional bouts of fever and other ailments all babies routinely suffer from, Arjun was growing into a healthy and happy boy.

The work load at the office kept on increasing in spite of the entire division working long hours and Anand was finding lesser time to spend freely at home. He frequently went abroad for more business, often for weeks together. He went to Singapore two more times but thankfully did not run into Nikita or anyone else there. In any case his home and office were intoxicating enough for him not to think of the past.

Asha, though, began feeling the distance creeping in between her and Anand who was not available for more than a few days at a stretch. Prosperity and success came to them at a price she found too high but had to pay nevertheless. In spite of the sheer joy of bringing up Arjun, Asha was missing Anand very much and pined for his exclusive company. Anand too pined for Asha, but just could not spend enough time with her now.

That old habits die hard is an adage needing no proof. It was true in Anand's case too. Somewhere along during the frequent trips abroad, Anand found vent to his stress and loneliness in the compelling company of an attractive woman he met at a social gathering with some clients. Strangely, Anand did not suffer the pangs of guilt like he did with Nikita in Singapore. Instead, he ended up having a very long and loving chat with Asha much to her ignorant delight. Back home, he strangely found his love and longing for Asha grow even stronger and thoroughly enjoyed this feeling of guiltless rejuvenation.

For Anand, both his domestic and business lives were at their blissful best. And he basked in them, unaware and unmindful of how long this bliss would last.

# 18

The cryptic police summons said it all:

Mister Anand,

You are hereby requested to attend the office of the undersigned during office hours within four days from receipt of this summons in connection with a police inquiry into the death of an Indian citizen Ms. NIKITA RAO during her domicile abroad in Singapore. Your cooperation in this regard will be appreciated.

Yours truly,

RANJAN CHOWDHURY IPS

Asst Commissioner of Police

Neither Anand nor his father was in town when the summons were delivered at the North Star Corporation. Mrs. Narmada too was on leave and Anand's assistant thought it best take it to the boss's home. Asha was in the midst of an e-mail session with an overseas client and it wasn't until a few hours later that she got to read the summons.

This must be a police blunder, Asha first thought. Anand

could never be involved in a woman's death, she assured herself. The North Star address however was unmistakable and the incident had occurred in Singapore where Anand went regularly. Asha had to call Anand at once wherever he was.

"Anand! Can you hear me?" Asha shouted into the phone

"Sorry darling, the line is very feeble. Is everything OK there, dear?"

"No Anand, we have a problem!" Asha's voice continued to be feeble. On Anand's advice she disconnected and he called back at once.

"What is it, Asha?"

"Anand, do you know any girl by name Nikita Rao?"

". . ." Asha's query baffled Anand

"Anand, did you hear me?" Asha repeated her question

". . . I used to know her a long time ago, darling. Why do you ask?"

"She's dead, Anand!" Asha's voice came through clearly

"Dead? How do you know?" Anand was shocked and confused

"There's a police summons for you, that's how! Who's Nikita Rao, Anand? How do you know her? And for how long?" Asha sounded very upset and Anand could understand why

"Asha, listen! I'm back home the day after tomorrow. We can talk in detail then, OK?" Anand didn't wait to find out if it was OK, he just hung up.

The moment Anand reached home two days later, Asha hastily ushered him into their room. With Arjun fast asleep, Asha got right to the point by showing Anand the summons.

"Anand! What is this mess? Why didn't you tell me you knew this girl?"

"Asha! I knew so many girls here and in USA, before marriage. That doesn't mean anything! Take it easy and let me handle this, OK?" Quickly recovering from the initial shock abroad, Anand had then and there decided to be neither defensive nor frank. He was grimly aware that unless handled cleverly Nikita's ghost was bound to break open his pre-marital Pandora's Box.

"Anand, you just got a police summons concerning a woman's death and you want me to take it easy? I'm coming with you to the police station tomorrow, that's for sure!" Asha's nervousness began to blur Anand's thoughts

"Are you crazy, Asha? A police station is the last place someone like you should go to! It's just a summons, for heaven's sake. I'm not a suspect, OK? All they can do is ask me a few questions. Calm down now, will you?"

"But Anand..."

"Don't argue, Asha! You're not coming with me! I'll come back and replay what happens there to your heart's content! Let's forget this and join Dad & Mom for dinner, OK?" Anand thus managed to quell the brewing storm for the day. Anand's agitated mind was now focussed on how to handle the police.

When Anand finally fell asleep that night, he dreamed of Asha and two policemen breaking into the room where Anand had pinned down a screaming Nikita to the bed. Just when Anand's free hand grabbed a knife lying nearby, the door gave way and one of the policemen opened fire with a Sten gun. Anand jerked out of his nightmare, only to realise it was his bedside alarm.

# 19

The long wait in ACP Ranjan Chowdhury's office was driving Anand mad but he kept himself busy with calls to the office. Just when Anand was giving up hope of meeting the ACP a handsome man in his mid-thirties dressed in impeccable khakhi walked in exuding confidence. The interrogation commenced right away over coffee served by an orderly appearing from nowhere.

"Mr. Chowdhury, how on earth did you link me with this case? I mean, how did you conclude I knew the dead girl at all?" Anand wanted an answer even before the interrogation began

"That's police work for you, Mr. Anand!" the ACP quipped and sensing his curiosity explained "Singapore police reached the dead girl's place and found this note near her body" Ranjan Chowdhury gave Anand a paper which he fished out from the case file "She obviously wrote it before taking sleeping pills with alcohol" Anand hardly recognised Nikita's scribbling but could clearly visualise her resorting to this desperation as he read the suicide note:

"Dearest Anand,

I'm not sure if this note will reach you at all. You are the only person who meant anything to me, all the more after my father passed away. After our night at your hotel, I promised myself not to bother you again. I tried to find another man like you suggested. But there is no one else like you. I find no point in carrying on with this miserable life without you. If all that crap about rebirth is true I want to be born as your wife next time. God bless you meanwhile. PS: Sorry if this note gets you into trouble with Asha" Though he knew it was futile to do so, Anand wished fervently that this whole episode would dissolve like all nightmares do.

"But this happened in Singapore! How come our police are involved?" Anand's naiveté amused the ACP

"Come on Mr. Anand, you surprise me! They traced your address from your hotel and sent the case file to us through Interpol. Nikita is an Indian citizen, remember?" The ACP clarified

"I see. What next, Mr. Chowdhury? Am I a suspect or something?" Anand's anxiety made the ACP laugh aloud

"Of course not, Mr. Anand! This is a suicide, remember? We need some details from you about the dead girl, that's all"

"How can you be so sure it's me? Anand could be anyone!" Anand resorted to last minute logic

"Sure, it can mean anyone. But the hotel register has your name as well as your address. The receptionists remember the girl leaving several messages for you with them. The suicide note mentions the name Asha. We checked out that your wife's name is Asha. Want more proof, Mr. Anand?" Ranjan Chowdhury responded politely

"What more proof do you have anyway, Mr. Chowdhury?" Anand was now curious to know

"These articles" the ACP said as he reached for a cardboard box inside his desk and handed it over to Anand "Please examine them, Mr. Anand, but don't touch them!"

Though Anand recognised his gifts to Nikita, he tried being defiant "How can you be sure these . . ." but was interrupted by the ACP

"All we need to do is match your fingerprints with those already on these articles. If you still insist on denying, that is!" Seeing Anand suddenly retreat into silence the ACP cajoled him "Mr. Anand, there is no need for any alarm or tension. All you have to do is to help us fill up blanks on the girl's background and your association with her! So we can close this file and move on to other cases. Now, shall we get on with it, Mr. Anand?"

Anand not only answered all the questions but also bared his heart to the ACP on Nikita. At the end of it all, Anand discovered he had found a friend in ACP Ranjan Chowdhury who in turn found Anand to be a vulnerable but decent man very much in love with his wife.

"I must admit I had a low opinion of policemen until today, Ranjan!"

"Seeing too many movies, Anand? They're just fiction. Fact is there are far more number of honest cops in the force than crooked ones. If it were not so, do you think I'd stick to this uniform? Anyway, I'm so happy I met you today" The ACP's affection came through genuinely

"The pleasure is all mine, Ranjan. I've found myself a friend!"

"So have I, Anand!"

"As soon as you can, you're coming home to meet Asha and my parents. Who knows, they may even find a bride for you!" Anand quipped in happiness "But, Ranjan, remember my request about Asha not to be . . ."

"Anand, trust me. You think I'm stupid to let your wife know anything? Now, forget this case and go home. I'll catch up with you soon" The ACP's assurance relieved Anand of his anxiety completely as he drove home to relieve Asha of hers.

# 20

"Dearest Anand,

...... You are the only person who meant anything to me, .
........ After our night at your hotel, .................
........ But there is no one else like you. .......... I want
to be born as your wife next time. .......... PS: Sorry if this
note gets you into trouble with Asha"

As she read and re-read these sentences, Asha felt the ground
slip away from under her feet. She now cursed herself for
having pressurised Sekhar to get for her the Nikita case details
using whatever influence he had with the police. But what else
could she have done when Anand was being so secretive? It
was obvious to Asha that Anand concealed a lot more than he
revealed and sheer concern for Anand drove her to get to the
bottom of the matter. Sekhar tried his best to keep the suicide
note away from Asha, but he was bulldozed into getting it not
just by Asha but Sulekha too.

With one stroke of her pen Nikita had turned her world upside
down, Asha realised, as she debated within herself what to
do next. Othello's agony over Desdemona on stage now
tormented Asha for real. Her psyche was torn between a wife

very much in love with her husband and a woman refusing to ignore this brutal assault on her ego!

That Anand and his father were both away on tour when Asha got hold of Nikita's note helped her make her decision of shifting to her brother's place first. Anand's mother, blissfully unaware of the situation, readily accepted Asha's request of visiting her mother. But she insisted Arjun remain with her to keep her company and Asha couldn't but relent.

While her brother was thrilled on Asha's maiden visit to his home, her mother had immediately sensed that something was amiss. Not yet ready to bare her heart, Asha painted a happy picture to her mother. She took both of them out to dinner where Sulekha joined them. It was late in the night when they returned home and her brother went straight to bed. Asha sat in the living room with her mother to watch television.

"What's wrong, Asha?" Asha's mother enquired innocuously

"What do you mean? What could be wrong, mother?" Asha parried

"You should know, you tell me! You didn't come here for a holiday. Is it to do with your in-laws or with Anand? You can tell me, that's what mothers are always there for!" Her mother took Asha into her arms

The pent up humiliation and agony inside Asha burst like a dam as she broke down in her mother's embrace. It took her mother all her tact to learn what had happened and all her patience to console Asha who finally fell asleep in her mother's lap.

"Daddy, mummy go to big mummy house!" Arjun announced as Anand unpacked and showered him with toys he invariably brought from every tour

"Big mummy is here.   Where is your mummy?" Anand enquired casually, disappointed on not seeing Asha

"Not this big mummy, that big mummy!" Arjun clarified succinctly

"OK darling, let's go meet that big mummy" Anand carried Arjun to the kitchen where his mother was supervising lunch preparations.

"Asha went to visit her mother, Anand.  I kept Arjun with me to give Asha a break from babysitting" Anand's mother informed him as she took Arjun into her lap

"OK, mom.  I'll go pick her up after lunch" Anand said eagerly

"No, you won't!  Let her spend some more time with her mother, it's been a long time.  You can bring her back this weekend, that'll give her at least two more days.  Take Arjun with you when you go there and spend two days with them yourself" Anand's mother instructed him

"Two more days without Asha?  Impossible!" thought Anand as he nodded to his mother but decided to bring her back the next day itself

"Big mummy!" Arjun screamed in joy as Asha's mother received them at the door.  After blessing Anand who touched her feet, Asha's mother grabbed Arjun and carrying him to her room she said "Asha is in her room there, go right in" Anand hurried to Asha's room and yanked open the door

"Can't you knock before coming in?" Asha shouted and hurriedly finished dressing on seeing who it was "Where are your manners?"

"Take it easy! If I can't barge in, who else can?" Anand retorted as he grabbed Asha fondly but she pushed him away indignantly

"Hey! What's the matter with you today?" Anand tried to grab her again but in vain as she walked away from him and sat on the bed "Is this how you receive your beloved husband after ten days?"

". . ." seething with anger, Asha remained silent

"Come on, Asha. Is it something I said or did?" Anand began to feel hurt

". . ."

"Come on Asha! Speak up, will you?" Anand was now irritated

". . ." Asha refused to be drawn into conversation

"Asha, I'm serious. What's wrong with you? Why don't you talk to me?"

"......"

"Open your mouth, dammit!" Anand was outright angry now "Want me to call your mother in to make you talk?" Anand shouted as he yanked the door open and stepped out of the room

"Come in and close the door! And keep mother and everyone else out of this!" Asha's harsh tone stunned Anand into quickly shutting the door

"Keep everyone out of what?" Anand asked anxiously

"Out of our miserable life, that's what!" Asha said without looking up

"Miserable? Couldn't you stop playing games and tell me what this is all about?" Anand asked in astonishment

"It's about the games you've been playing with me!"

"What do you mean? What games?" Anand was now worried

". . ."

"What game, dammit?" Anand was now very angry

"The game called Nikita" Asha said finally "Remember?"

"What's there to remember? I thought it's a closed chapter!" Anand wondered where this conversation was leading to

"It just got reopened, Anand! I saw the note she left you!" Asha said looking directly into Anand's eyes

". . ." it was now Anand's turn to remain silent as he groped for words "How did you . . . anyway she's dead and gone! What's the point of raking it up now? We should be thinking of our future!"

"Our future, Mister Anand, is a thing of the past!" Asha retorted

"Stop overreacting, Asha! Don't let such a small matter spoil what we have!" Anand pleaded but without hope

"Small matter? Cheating on your wife is a small matter for you?" Anand's words infuriated Asha further

"I'm sorry, Asha. What I meant was . . ." Anand became defensive

"Anand, will you please do me a favour?"

"Anything for you Asha, anything on earth!" Anand was encouraged by the softening of Asha's tone

"Will you please get out of my room? And out of my life?"

"Listen, Asha! Now don't get over emotional!" Anand was stupefied by her words "We can sort this thing out, trust me!"

"Trust you? Never again! Now, will you please leave?" Asha said firmly

"Asha, please! I'm sorry I hurt you but I never meant to. Don't be so inhuman!" Anand appealed to her

"Don't waste your time with an inhuman person like me! Please leave!"

"Please Asha, I said I'm sorry, I really am! I'm will go down on my knees, if you want me to but please. . ." Anand was almost in tears

"Anand! If you don't leave right now, I will!" Asha, too outraged to relent, got up from the bed to leave the room

"OK, Asha! I'll leave!" Anand felt miserable as he stormed out of the room "But I'll be back!"

Asha's mother was too busy in the kitchen preparing food to notice Anand picking up Arjun from her room and leaving without telling her. Asha remained in her room, unaware that Arjun had come and that Anand took him back.

Anand did not want to go home. He went on a long drive to the beach. The same beach, he realised, where he often took Nikita. Arjun fell asleep en route and Anand walked alone for hours along the shore before returning to his car. How lucky kids are, Anand thought, seeing his son still asleep "God, why can't you send a tidal wave now and end this ordeal for me?" Anand cried aloud as he got into his car. God did answer his cry, but only with heavy rain that lashed the city for the rest of the night.

# 21

"Anand"

". . ." In spite of the acrimony that had crept into their relationship Asha's voice sounded as sweet as ever, only Anand hated to admit it now

"Anand, are you listening?" As if I have a choice! Anand thought and said curtly

"Yes, I'm listening. What is it about?"

"You know what it's about . . . Arjun"

"Arjun? What about him? He's quite happy here!" Anand replied curtly

"That's not for you alone to decide! We must meet. Can you come over?"

"No Asha! Let's meet here at home. Have you forgotten how you treated me last time I was there?" Anand was defiant

"The same way you treated me, Anand, but no point in going into that" Asha was equally defiant "Let's meet at a place where we can talk this out. How about Sekhar's place?"

Anand wanted to tell Asha to go to hell but accepted to meet her, not wanting to prolong the confrontation.

Anand just could not get over the humiliation, first at Asha's place and later that night at home during the confession to his father in private.

"Anand, I had warned you about this at the very beginning, didn't I? This was why I was never in favour of this marriage, knowing your ways. Which girl would tolerate a philandering husband? Certainly not a middle class girl like Asha. Now, we all pay the price!" His father's admonishing only compounded the humiliation

"Dad, I already have Asha against me. At least you and mom should be on my side now instead of. . ." Anand broke off with tears rolling down his eyes, compelling his father to embrace him

"Now who said we're not on your side? It's just that I'm as hurt as you are. And how do you think your mom will feel? Boy, I wish you had behaved yourself!" Anand's father continued but in a softened tone

"Dad, you know how much I have changed since my marriage. But this is something out of the blue, from the past! I don't know how Asha got hold of that suicide note. I didn't tell her anything. Nor did that ACP who interrogated me. Bad luck, Dad, just bad luck!"

"Boy, what a royal mess!" Anand's father lamented

"Dad, can't we keep mom out of this?" Anand appealed

"How? She'll come to know anyway. Leave that to me. You go talk to Asha and bring her back home. I'm sure she loves you enough to forgive you" Anand wished he could share his Dad's optimism

"I'm not sure Dad. She's one hell of a girl. You should have seen the way she reacted!" Anand confessed

"Go down on your knees, if you have to! It's your fault, remember?"

"What do you think I did this morning, Dad? It just didn't work then and it won't work now. OK, it's my fault but what more can I do? Kill myself? Dad, I hope at least you and mom are on my side!" Anand's agony disturbed his father too

"Anand dear, stop talking like a child! Of course we're on your side, where's the doubt? But first think of how bad Asha must be feeling. You owe that much to her. She's your wife, and a great one at that!" Anand's father left him to break the bad news to his wife

Anand had decided to skip the meeting with Asha but changed his mind after talking to his father. As he went to bed that night, Anand watched an English movie he had already seen several times on DVD - *Kramer v/s Kramer* - in which Dustin Hoffman and Meryl Streep play separated parents fighting for custody of their only son in court.

"Anand v/s Anand"... that's what the court would call their case for Arjun's custody, Anand mused as he fell asleep.

# 22

"Asha!" Sekhar called out as he saw Anand's car halt outside his house "Anand is here"

Asha came out of one of the rooms followed by Sulekha from the kitchen carrying a tray filled with biscuits and coffee she set on the centre table in the living room. After a lot of deliberations the previous day, the three of them decided that once Anand arrived Sekhar would proceed to his office as usual while Sulekha would be around, just in case Asha needed her, but would remain out of sight.

After formal greetings were exchanged and Sulekha forced a coffee cup into his hands, Anand was left alone with Asha. The silence was so palpable Anand could almost touch it. Asha waited for Anand to finish his coffee and got straight to the point.

"Arjun needs a mother more than a father right now, I hope you'll agree" Asha said succinctly, not wanting to prolong this meeting

When he arrived, Anand was hoping he could talk Asha into coming back home and was ready with his words of apology.

But her body language and blunt tone ruffled his bruised ego further, so he decided to let go.

"I don't agree! Why should he have to choose between you and me? Can't you think of our families and forget what has happened?" Anand demanded

"Did you think of our families when you took that woman to your room? Why should I now?" Asha reacted exactly as Anand guessed she would

"It won't happen again, Asha, I promise! There's no point in talking of the past, is there?" Anand pleaded, fighting his ego

"To me, there's no point in talking of the present! I respect myself too much to live with someone who doesn't care for me!"

"How can you ever say that? Haven't I cared for you more than anyone else in the world? OK I made a big mistake, I'm really, truly very sorry! But does that make my love for you any less genuine?" Anand spoke from his heart but the words just didn't reach Asha's

"Strange way of showing your love! Remember the book you gave me when we met the first time after Singapore . . . Love Story?"

"I remember. What about it?" Asha's query took Anand by surprise

"Love is never having to say you're sorry! That you didn't remember!"

". . ." Anand was taken aback for a while then asked angrily "What do you want me to do now, Asha? Go down on my knees and beg you to forgive me and come back? I'm ready to do that if that's what you want!" Anand's burst out

"If that's what I wanted, I would have had it by now!" Asha replied calmly "but what I want is my freedom, my dignity, and yes, I want Arjun's custody!" Asha couldn't have been more precise

"And what if I don't give him to you? What if I go to court?" Anand waited for Asha to be taken aback but she didn't oblige

"I would go to court too! I would also conclude that you are pig headed!" Asha retorted

"Pig headed? What do you mean?" Anand was indignant

"Courts are only for those who are too pig headed to see reason and fairness by themselves! I hope you are at least sensible, if not sincere!" Asha's reasoning struck Anand like an arrow

"So let's be reasonable and fair, shall we?" Anand tried to seize the initiative "Don't you think Arjun will be safer and more secure with me and my affluent parents than with you and your sick mother?"

"As long as you remain Arjun's father only, yes. But what happens when you have other children? Your parents won't let you remain single for long, that's for sure!" Asha argued

"That holds good for you too! You could marry again and have kids, couldn't you?" Anand countered her logic

"Thanks to you, that's one thing in life I'll never do again! I can give it to you in writing, if it satisfies you"

"OK, so you tell me what we should do now!" Anand asked,

ignoring Asha's taunt "Shall I keep him for the weekends while you have him during the week?"

"It sounds logical, but not fair to Arjun. He's hardly three now, not old enough to shuttle between you and me every week. I feel he should remain with me until he finishes school" Asha reasoned

"And until then, what do I do? Look around for my next kid?" Anand quipped

"Arjun will spend all his vacations with you at your home" Asha replied, ignoring Anand's humour "that way, you don't have to worry about packing his lunch and searching for his socks every day! I think this makes the best sense for the three of us" Asha replied

"And after his schooling? What then?" Anand asked

"That's when you can use your affluence, for his higher studies. He will live with you and visit me during his vacations. What do you say, Anand? This way, no courtrooms, no dirty linen in public and no damage to family honour!" Asha concluded

And no "ANAND V/S ANAND" in court, Anand thought as he left Sekhar's place convinced by Asha's logic, disappointed with her refusal to forgive him and daunted by the task of making his parents see sense in this arrangement.

# 23

Anand and Asha found the arrangement easy enough to accept themselves but not so easy to get their families to accept it. Asha's mother resented it, hopeful that Asha would eventually forgive Anand and return to him. Anand's mother was angry with Asha, finding her retribution too harsh. In contrast, Anand's father reconciled to the arrangement as being practical and workable, his only concern now being damage control. He decided on an explanation for Asha's absence from the office and their home: she had volunteered to relocate to America to personally handle a time bound contract their company was obliged to suddenly undertake. He also decided to persuade Asha to visit America and meet a few North Star clients whom she would handle herself. That the grapevine would eventually catch up with the truth was inevitable but immaterial to him. A façade of family vanity was only what could be achieved now, reasoned Anand's father.

Much to her mother's chagrin, Asha remained steadfast in not going back to Anand. After moving into her brother's apartment, Asha chose a decent school nearby for Arjun. At first she rejected the America idea but later found sense in it, seeing in it the breakthrough she needed in her life without

Anand. After a short trip to America where she picked up her first few independent contracts, Asha set up her office in a small apartment near her brother's.

Sekhar gave up hope of Asha's reunion with Anand but only after exhausting all his persuasive skills. He made Sulekha accompany Asha to America, a gesture that endeared him further to both the families. He motivated Asha to set up her own company and handled all her company matters himself.

To recover from the huge blow to his marital bliss Anand plunged himself into his work. He made himself busy enough not to pine for Asha or Arjun. He frequently went abroad for business and leisure, often mixing both. Hesitant at first, Anand gradually returned to his old ways this time for the sole objective of getting Asha's memories out of his mind. That he did not succeed was another matter.

At an age when toys, rhymes and playmates meant everything, Arjun enjoyed school as much as he did the pampering of his grandmother and uncle. Blissfully unaware of his parents' predicament, he thoroughly enjoyed his annual vacations at his father's home where it would become festival time for Anand and his parents. Parting time would be very tearful to Arjun but he would quickly return to the cocoon of his mother's world.

The wheels of time rolled on thus, very slowly.

# 24

The sea turned dark and angry as the sun disappeared for its daily rest. The breeze was cool and comforting to all others on the beach except for Anand, who stood brooding in the balcony of his cottage. In spite of the sensual company awaiting him inside, Anand felt lonely.

It was more than two years since Asha walked out on him. The only time he got to see her was at the beginning and the end of Arjun's vacations. Even then she hardly spoke to him and left after brief pleasantries with his parents. Apart from thinning down a little, she looked as good as ever. Her face did not betray any bitterness, only aloofness. His parents, however, were yet to come to terms with this embarrassing estrangement. Nor did Anand, for that matter.

Not in the mood to return to his half occupied double bed, Anand fondly reminisced on his last visit to this very resort with Asha just after the doctor confirmed her pregnancy.

"Anand!" an exhausted Asha whispered into an equally exhausted Anand's ear "Are you sure this is safe for the baby? I mean, shouldn't we be staying away from each other?"

"I thought you checked with Dr. Sheela and she said it's OK, didn't you?" Anand was suddenly conscious of the possible consequences but remained satiated nevertheless

"Doctor Sheela told me to be careful from the fifth month onwards, so I guess it's OK for another month. But after that, you'd better stay away from me or I'll have to shift to my mother's place!" Asha said

"Another month, meaning another thirty nights! Thank God for that . . . and dear doctor Sheela!" Anand quipped

"Anand, I wonder what you'll do from next month!" Asha asked tauntingly

"What do you mean what I'll do?" Anand failed to grasp what Asha meant. Only on seeing Asha's mischievous smile did he understand

"Oh, I know what I'll do! I'll get a beautiful new secretary at the office. When I'm tired of her, I'll go to Las Vegas! If I'm still not . . ."

Anand's mouth was abruptly shut by what he first thought were Asha's slender fingers, but when he realised they were her lips he savoured them until Asha withdrew them out of breathlessness.

"Anand" Asha said amidst gasps "you are Mr. Devil, you know that?"

"And you are my Miss India, Miss Las Vegas and Miss Universe!"

"Correction . . . Mrs. Universe!" Asha frolicked "Now, will

you ever start thinking of returning home? I'm already feeling homesick"

"Now you sound like Mrs. Devil. Anyway, whatever a pregnant devil says! We'll leave the day after tomorrow" Anand said lazily

"So you can have one more night?" Asha said as she got out of bed

"Two, actually! What about the rest of tonight?" Anand pulled her back into bed

"Mr. Devil"


"Anand darling!" the shrill voice from inside the cottage rudely shook Anand out his trance "What are you doing out there?"

"Wondering what I'm doing out here with you!" Anand wanted to shout but instead said "Waiting for a call from my office. The signal's weak inside the room"

"But darling, your cell phone is lying here on the bed!"

Anand first cursed Asha for turning his excursion sour and then himself for being forgetful "Asha, you Devil! You walked out on me but haven't left me alone. Either come back to me or kill me!" Anand fumed silently as he dragged his reluctant feet and heart back into the cottage.

# 25

After an unusually turbulent flight the airplane landed smoothly on the tarmac. But Asha's mind remained turbulent even as she made her way through Singapore Customs and headed for her hotel. Thankfully for her, it wasn't the same hotel she had shared with Anand twice.

This was the first Singapore trip Asha had to undertake alone. She wanted very much to bring Arjun along, but his school made that impossible. She was apprehensive of leaving him alone with her mother. Ever since Arjun returned home after his vacation a month ago, he had become inquisitive and often asked awkward questions concerning his father, especially at bedtime. Asha was never evasive in her replies, though the sheer pain of recollecting the past was what she hated most.

"Mrs. Asha Anand!" the receptionist said politely "Your room key, madam" Oddly, Asha felt comfortable being addressed by the name she had checked in with by sheer habit. As she settled down in her room for the day, she could not help drifting back to the exhilarating memories of her honeymoon in this very city.

"Asha!" Anand's voice did not reach Asha who was under the shower after a tiresome journey

"Asha, can you hear me?" This time his voice was loud enough for Asha to stop the shower and listen

"Anand, I can't hear you. Hold on for a minute, will you?" Asha shouted back as she dried herself

"Now tell me" Asha asked as she came out of the bathroom, fresh as dew

"If you are planning any sightseeing, forget it! We're not going to stir out of the room. We'll have all our meals here, get that?"

"I get that, but I doubt if the hotel will" Asha was curious "I mean what if they break into our room, thinking we're dead?"

"We are in the Honeymoon Penthouse, remember? We even have a swimming pool out there on the terrace, so we don't have to step out for anything at all!" Anand clarified with a flourish

"And what if I felt like shopping? I hear Singapore is full of shopping malls"

"And what would you shop for?" Anand asked

"Clothes, of course!"

"Clothes? My dear Mrs Asha Anand, the last thing a girl should be wearing on her honeymoon is clothes! Do you think I'll let you wear any clothes at all on this trip?" Anand announced with a smile

"Anand!" Asha protested "Behave yourself, we're amidst civilised people!"

"People? Where? Show me one person!" Anand asked

"Look here! Not one but a few hundred!" Asha located the TV remote and switched on a news channel showing a gathering of delegates at a UNO seminar

"So you want to take our honeymoon to the United Nations, even before it has begun?" Anand asked in mock seriousness

"Not if you allow me to wear my clothes" Asha retorted laughing loudly "After all, it's the fundamental right of a woman!"

"And what about fundamental rights of husbands on their honeymoon?" Anand persisted

"Thankfully, husbands on honeymoon are not the concern of the UNO! Now, before we get into a human rights dispute, let's eat. I'm starving!"

"I'll call room service. I'm starving too . . . for you!"


"Room service madam! Your food order" The attendant broke into Asha's thoughts. He parked the food trolley and left

Though she did not admit it, Asha knew the real cause for the turbulence in her mind . . . Anand! "If only he had stayed away from that woman, life would have been so beautiful today" Asha thought and then admonished herself "What's happening to me? He doesn't deserve even a passing thought after what he did to me. And here I am constantly thinking of him. Do I still love him? How can it be, when I hate him so much? God, save me from this torture!"

But the torture would resume when Asha returned to her room

after work every day. While her heart pined for Anand, her ego stood like a wall between them. At the end of the trip Asha resolved never to travel alone again and suffer this pain. Asha knew very well where the remedy for this pain lay, but acknowledging it was something she just could not do.

# 26

Anand was in the middle of a brainstorming session in the conference hall where he was interrupted by a phone call from Sekhar.

"Anand!" Sekhar sounded very sober "Can I talk to you for a minute?"

"Well . . ." Anand was tempted to ask Sekhar to call later but thought the better of it "Go ahead, Sekhar. How's life?"

"I've got some bad news for you . . ."

"Oh, my God! Please don't tell me something's happened to Asha. Please!" Anand panicked within himself "What is it?" he asked Sekhar

"Asha's mother passed away! Half an hour back. Multiple organ failure"

". . ." though hugely relieved, Anand felt very sorry for Asha "Where are they right now?"

"They're bringing her home from the hospital. Cremation is in the evening. I thought I'd inform you immediately"

"Of course, Sekhar. Thank you. Dad and mom would also

want to come. I'll be there in an hour" Anand broke up the meeting and rushed home

The assortment of vehicles outside the residential complex was indicative of the crowd assembled inside Asha's flat. More than half the visitors were North Star staff who stood at attention on seeing Anand and his father. The rest seemed to be Asha's own staff. Sulekha was holding Arjun in her lap while her hand clasped Asha's. Sekhar was helping Asha's brother in the ceremony that was in progress.

Asha broke down in the arms of Anand's mother who consoled her silently. After laying a garland at the feet of the departed soul, Anand's father sat in a corner, quietly acknowledging the salutes of his staff present. On seeing Anand, Arjun ran into his arms and remained there throughout.

It was late in the evening by the time the obsequies and the cremation were completed and they all returned home. Anand's father left from the crematorium, while his mother remained with Asha. She advised Anand to take Arjun home with him. Asha was too much in grief to object. Her brother silently packed Arjun's clothes for one week.

"Asha . . ." Anand fumbled for words "I'm very sorry. Your mother really was a great lady . . . be brave for your brother's sake" he said

". . . ." Asha nodded silently

"And don't worry about Arjun. We're all there to look after him" he assured

"And who's there to look after me? I'm an orphan now!"

Asha wanted to cry out aloud as she watched Anand leave with Anand

The bell rang as soon as Asha closed the front door. It was Anand again.

"Asha, I don't know how to say this but mom and I very much want you to come home. At least until you feel better, OK?"

"My brother is all alone, how can I leave him?" Asha replied

"I'm all alone too, but haven't you left me?" Anand wanted to yell at her "I understand. Take care, Asha" he said

"You too. Take care!" Asha wanted to say but all she managed to mumble was "Send Arjun back in a week. He'll miss school"

"I'm missing my whole life, Asha! Why don't you come back? Please!" Anand screamed to himself before saying "Sure, Asha. Whatever you wish"

"Whatever I wish? I wish you never met that woman! I wish you never took her to your room! I wish you never made me do what I'm doing now to both of us! I wish . . ." Asha interrupted her own thoughts with a feeble "Thanks"

Asha stood in the balcony and waved her hand at the car that sped away. She saw a hand waving back at her. Arjun, she guessed "or could it be Anand beckoning me to come back?" she wondered.

That night sleep just didn't come to Asha. If it wasn't her mother's memories, it was Anand's thoughts that were tormenting her "Why? What have I done to deserve this pain?" Asha asked herself repeatedly until sleep condescended on her just before dawn.

# 27

"Is this an international airport or a *kumbh mela*?" Anand fretted as he looked around for a slot in the car park, which he finally found after an exasperating search. He then braced himself for a long wait for the British Airways flight from London to arrive.

"Anand" it was one of those rare calls from mother to his office that afternoon "please come straight home from office today. I have an important work for you" mother was always brief on the phone, Anand thought

"Sure, mom" Anand assured her wondering what this important work could be

"Do you remember Archana?" His mother asked Anand over tea as soon as he reached home

"Archana? No, I don't" Anand admitted

"What's the matter with you? Archana, your London uncle's daughter!"

"Oh yes, Archana! Now I remember"

"She's arriving from London tonight. You have to pick her up"

"Why me? I don't know her at all. I don't even know how she looks, mom!" Anand pleaded

"That's exactly why I want you to pick her up! You two must get to know each other well" his mother said suppressing a smile

"Get to know each other? What for, mom?"

"Shouldn't you get to know the girl you will be sharing your life with?" Anand's mother revealed succinctly

"Mom, is this some kind of a joke? What do you mean sharing my life with?" Anand was taken aback

"Come on Anand, you know what I mean. How long do you think you're going to live like a hermit? Who's going to be with you when your father & I are not around? It's high time you found another girl. And who better for all of us than Archana?" Anand's mother reasoned

"Are you out of your mind, mom? I'm a married man for God's sake!"

"Are you, Anand? I'm not sure anymore. Not since she walked out on you!"

"Oh, so now it's she, eh? Not Asha anymore?" Anand asked furiously

"I have all the regard for her, Anand. But I'm a mother first and my son comes first for me. I can't see you suffer like this anymore!"

"And you think my suffering will end if I marry again?"

"At least it won't make you unhappier than you are now" suddenly Anand's father butted in "Besides, it will give a lot of happiness and pride to our family. And God knows we badly need both now!" and the argument continued

"Dad, how can I marry again when I'm already married?"

"What do all other men like you do? Get a divorce, dammit!"

"Divorce?" Anand reacted as if he was hit by a load of bricks "So mom and you have already declared my marriage null and void, have you Dad?"

"Anand, it's high time you stopped being a lovelorn husband and became a responsible son. Your life with Asha is finished! The sooner you realise this, the better for all of us. Now, go pick up Archana from the airport. Whether you get to like her or not, she's our guest. Now go!"

In spite of three cappuccinos, Anand felt tired and depressed. At long last Anand was relieved to see London passengers trickling out of the arrival gate. His mother could only show him pictures of a younger Archana from the family album, so Anand felt it wise to carry a placard with her name on it.

"Hi, Anand!" the shrill voice that greeted him was that of a tall, slim and very attractive girl dressed in typically western attire. Before he could react, Archana greeted him with a bear hug "My! You've grown tall and handsome since I last remember seeing you. I'm Archana!"

"Hello, Archana! Welcome to India" was all that Anand could manage to say, confused as he was between his first impressions of this warm and lively cousin of his and the actual purpose of her visit.

The conversation in the car was dominated by Archana whom Anand found to be a warm person with abundant love for life. By the time they reached home he felt surprisingly relaxed in his cousin's presence. Anand watched amusedly as Archana touched his parents' feet and they in turn greeted their niece with bear hugs. They together enjoyed a hearty meal and heartier conversations till the wee hours.

That night Anand dreamt of being in an amusement park desperately trying to rescue Asha trapped in a giant wheel gone out of control. Finally when the giant wheel came to a halt there was no sign of Asha. Seated inside was Archana.

# 28

Of his own volition Anand decided to take the week off. His mother's delight knew no bounds on seeing Anand accompany Archana wherever she chose to go, without any coercion. She began dreaming of the wedding that soon would be the talk of the town.

After a delicious lunch of Indian cuisine, Anand took Archana on a long drive to his favourite leisure spot, the beach outside the city. Only a handful of cars were there in spite of it being a Sunday. Anand could not keep pace with Archana as she ran towards the sea. After more than an hour of splashing and screaming in the water, they dropped themselves on the sand exhausted.

"Archana" Anand called her attention "Are you enjoying yourself?"

"Of course I am, thank you very much" Archana's happiness was visible

"I need to talk to you Archana. About . . ."

"About us you mean? Go ahead. I'm listening" Archana was all ears

"Do you know, Archana? That our parents want us to get married?"

"Yes, I know. My father has been dreaming about nothing but my marriage, especially after his own marriage with mother broke up two years ago. Your mother is the only family he's got, you know. He is very fond of you, Anand" Archana said earnestly

"And you, Archana? Are you fond of me too?"

"Well, yes! I am beginning to be"

"Fond enough to spend the rest of your life with me?" Anand probed

". . ."

"You haven't answered me, Archana"

"I know my father will be happy. That means a lot to me, Anand"

"And what about your own happiness, Archana? Doesn't that mean anything to you?" Anand was now determined to know

"What's the matter, Anand? Aren't you happy about it?" It was Archana's turn to probe

"My being happy or not isn't important, your being is! Do you know I'm already married. . .for the last four years?"

"Yes. I was told you were once married to some woman who walked out on you"

"Some woman? I'm still married to that woman! Do you know why she walked out on me?" Anand was suddenly angry but not sure on whom

"I don't know, Anand. I don't care too, really! Why should I?" Archana asked

"Why? My dear Archana, because you want to share the rest of your life with me, that's why!" Anand was aghast at Archana's nonchalance

"What I want to share with you is our future, Anand, not your past! Past is past, isn't it?" Archana reasoned

"That's what you think! That's what I thought too! Till I learnt otherwise with Asha" Anand said pensively

"Asha?" Archana asked

"My wife! Whom I still love very much. Let me tell you how much!"

Anand took Archana on a journey of his surreal life with Asha, with all the love and pain in his heart. It was late evening but an engrossed Archana did not notice the time, not even the noisy crowds that thronged the beach by then.

"Do you know what it is like? To be rejected by someone you love more than yourself?"

". . ." Archana was silent for a while and then opened up "I never told this to anyone, but I will tell you. Yes, I do know what it is like, I've been through it myself! But not here, it's getting dark. Let's stop at some restaurant and I'll tell you all about it!"

And Archana told Anand all about it. How she fell in love with an Indian boy in her Kensington neighbourhood. How she finished school and college along with him. How she got engaged to him in the presence of their families. How on the day of the wedding the boy just disappeared along with his parents. How her parents, especially her father, began taking this ignominy to heart. How humiliating she herself found it to live with the jilt and deceit. How, on top of it all, her mother walked out on them for reasons known only to her. How her attempt to end her life, though foiled by her father, shattered him completely. How finally she agreed to visit India solely for the sake of her father's happiness.

"I don't know what to say, Archana!" a flabbergasted Anand consoled a shattered Archana "I feel sorry for you, really! If it's any solace, I'm always there for you . . . as your friend!"

"Thank you, Anand. I feel relieved now" Archana held Anand's hand firmly "And I'm always there for you too, my friend!"

It was only when the waiter remained standing at their table that they realised it was almost midnight and well beyond closing time. Back home both of them noticed the smiles exchanged between Anand's parents on seeing them, but they were too tired to correct their mistaken thinking.

# 29

In contrast to North Star Corporation, Asha's office was small in size, spartan in decor, simple in ambience but nevertheless equally bustling with activity. Twelve employees worked almost round the clock to meet crazy deadlines set by a steadily bulging clientele. At the centre of this bustle was Asha who endeared herself to clients and colleagues alike as an erudite professional and an empathic employer. Asha herself found work to be an anaesthetic that immunised her mind and heart from depression. Only when at work could she forget the emptiness in her life that until recently was filled with love and joy.

It was to be another busy afternoon for Asha who had just entered office after meeting a client. She was about to settle down to work when her mobile phone sprang into life to announce an unknown caller.

"Is that Mrs Asha, please?" a pleasant and exotic female voice asked

"Yes, it's me. May I know who's calling?" Asha replied with typical politeness

"My name is Archana. I've been referred to you by an associate of mine in London from where I've come from. I have business to discuss and I wonder if you could be so kind as to meet me at the Sheraton?" There was no mistaking the English etiquette in her voice

"Now?" Asha asked, raring to get into her work

"Yes! I'm afraid I have very little time in India. We could discuss it over lunch. Could I send my car to fetch you?"

"No, thanks. I'll meet you there in half an hour" Asha said as she grabbed her bag and rushed out

Meeting a new client always excited Asha as much as it made her nervous. Asha looked around the dimly lit restaurant for a single woman whom she finally found in a secluded corner.

"I'm Archana" the smile was arresting as was her presence

"Hello, I'm Asha. Welcome to India. Is this your first visit?" Asha enquired as she settled down facing Archana

"In the last fifteen years, yes. I was born here, though. I have family in this city with whom I'm staying" Archana spoke with grace and warmth "Mrs Asha, before we talk business could we get ourselves some food? I'm starving!"

"Sure, so am I!" Asha settled for a very simple meal and noticed that Archana did so too. By the time they were finished with the food they became friendly enough to discover they shared common tastes and similar attitudes

"How long are you in this business, Miss Archana?" Asha asked over fresh fruit juice

"You can skip the Miss and call me Archana. And Asha, to

be honest, I'm not in this business at all!" Archana blushed as she confessed

"I thought you wanted to discuss software business with me" Asha was confused "that's the only business I know"

"Actually, I came to discuss something else with you, Asha . . . your personal life, if I may!"

"I left a lot of work back at the office to meet you. What kind of a joke is this, Miss Archana?" Asha demanded

"No Miss, just Archana please! I am Anand's cousin from London. Anand, your husband" The revelation first shocked Asha then upset her

"In that case, Miss Archana, I'll say my goodbye now" Asha said "it was a pleasure doing business with you!" she added sarcastically as she rose from the table

"First, call me Archana! Next, give me fifteen minutes! And then, Asha, I'll accept your goodbye!" Archana laughed as she firmly pulled Asha back into her seat "Trust me, I don't intend to eat you! I've just had a good meal, thank you"

"If Anand thinks . . ." Asha couldn't complete her sentence

"Anand doesn't even know! I've come here on my own. I had to see you. And talk to you, Asha" Archana interrupted

"What's there to talk?" Asha refused to be drawn into the one subject she loathed "Whatever has happened is Anand's own doing. Shouldn't you be talking to him instead?"

"What do you think I've been doing these past five days, Asha?"

"And what does Anand have to say? That it's all my fault? That I am the one who's cruel and heartless to walk out on him?" Asha's indignation was apparent

"Calm down Asha, I'm on your side! I'm a woman too and know how it hurts when men behave the way they do" Archana said soothingly "Come, let's go to a more private and peaceful place" and surprisingly Asha found herself not resisting at all

They reached a park full of greenery but empty of people at this time of the day. Only yesterday Anand brought Archana to this park that simply was a miracle in the concrete jungle the city was. They settled down in the shade of a huge tree to resume their tête-à-tête.

"Do you know, Asha? It's only because of Anand that I'm sitting here with you, instead of sitting with him in a marriage hall!"

Archana explained in detail the purpose of her visit to India and the surprising discoveries she had made in the last few days. The tears rolling down Asha's cheeks assured Archana that love's labour was not lost for Anand after all. Whether Asha's ego would win or her heart was the only question remaining.

"If Anand's mother had her way, he would be seeking a divorce from you! And you would have given it to him on a rebound, wouldn't you?"

"And what if I give him this divorce now?" Asha's ego would not let go easily "At least his mother will be happy!"

"Will you be happy, Asha? You still love him, I can see!"

"Is love everything, Archana?" Asha demanded "Don't women deserve respect too? At least from themselves, if not from men?"

"Sure they do! But a husband, especially one who loves you, is different from all other men. You should know better than me, Asha!" Archana's reasoned

"Different enough to let him trample your ego?" Asha's hurt still showed

"What's ego doing in love? And in marriage? When you love a guy and marry him, you've already trampled your ego for him! At least you're married to someone like Anand. I trampled my ego for someone who trampled me in return and walked out!"

It was then that Archana revealed the secret of her aborted marriage in painful detail. Asha couldn't hold back her tears, nor could Archana. Embracing each other they cried aloud till their tears and throats dried up.

"Anand has already punished himself enough. Don't punish him any more, please!" Archana appealed as they reached Asha's home late in the evening "And don't punish yourself either, Asha! It's not even your fault!"

"Thanks, Archana. For everything!" Asha reciprocated "Anything at all I can do for you in return?"

"Return to Anand, before I return to London! That's the best thing you can do for me" Archana said with a bear hug "Good night, Asha"

Sleep eluded Asha as she rolled in bed with mixed feelings of agony and ecstasy, anger and excitement. It was almost dawn when Asha finally drifted into sleep. She was amidst angels dressed in white flying over sylvan countryside until they reached a lake with a gentle waterfall. As they descended, the waterfall revealed a cave with a brightly lit altar inside. As Asha stood hesitantly outside the cave, a veiled prince came out of the cave, kissed her hand and led her gently to the altar. As the veil lifted itself to reveal the smiling face of Anand, Asha woke out of her dream.

And woke up to what she had to do then.

# 30

*What makes human life go on eternally? What saves the human race from extinction on Earth?*

*Five Elements of Life . . . Air, Water, Fire, Earth & Sky?*

*Five Forces of Nature . . . Heat, Light, Sound, Electricity, Magnetism?*

*Food . . . undeniably the primary manifestation of Nature [or God]?*

*Music . . . that priceless gift of Nature that reins in the beast in Man?*

*Miracles of human intelligence . . . from the Wheel to the Super Computer, from visible rockets to Moon and Mars to invisible spy satellites that dot the sky?*

*Yes . . . all of these undoubtedly.*

*But above all else, what is most basic to human life on Earth is that natural, physical force of attraction between Man and Woman which is recognised, raved about, & revered universally as . . .* **LOVE** *!*

*Love between Man and Woman is an enigma that intrigues as much as it invigorates. Love and Hatred are two sides of the same coin, two shades of the same colour. Husbands, wives and lovers the world over will vouch for this, privately at least!*

Asha returned to Anand, even if she did not forgive him. Happily or not, they certainly lived together ever after.

*This maiden book of mine is a humble attempt to explore the esoteric world of man and woman in and out of love. I hope it was worth your leisure time.*

*With Love*

*Sukumar Mandalika*